The Secret WILD

The Secret WILD

ALEX EVELYN

First published 2022 by Walker Books Ltd
87 Vauxhall Walk, London SE11 5HJ

2 4 6 8 10 9 7 5 3 1

Text © 2022 Alex Evelyn

Cover and interior illustration © 2022 George Ermos

This book has been typeset in Berkeley Oldstyle, Beyond the Mountains, Botany,
Calligraserif, Cheddar Gothic Sans, Colporteur, Framboisier, Futura, Jellyka
CuttyCupcakes, Times Educational, Times New Roman and Uncle Edward

Printed and bound in Great Britain by CPI Group (UK) Ltd, Croydon CR0 4YY

British Library Cataloguing in Publication Data: a catalogue record for this
book is available from the British Library

ISBN 978-1-4063-9939-4

www.walker.co.uk

MIX
Paper from
responsible sources
FSC® C171272
FSC www.fsc.org

FOR MY PARENTS, JEAN AND ROGER,
FOR BEING SO VERY, VERY SPECIAL.

CHAPTER ONE

"Aren't you beautiful? I could hardly pass you by without a quick look, could I? Besides, those two are always in *such* a hurry."

The bird was no bigger than a cotton reel, its tiny wings beating a hundred times faster than a human heart to keep it airborne. As it dipped its long, curved beak in and out of a flower, it was watched by a girl with a frizzy halo of cinnamon-coloured hair. She reached quietly into the front pocket of her dungarees and her fingers settled on the hilt of a magnifying glass.

"Would you mind if I draw you? Don't tell *them* I was talking to you – they only think of you as something for scientific research. To them you're just a collection of chemical compounds, they can't imagine that you might have a personality too."

As she leaned in, magnifying glass to her eye, it wasn't the jewel-coloured feathers of the hummingbird that the girl was interested in, but the elegant scarlet trumpet flower the creature was taking its lunch from. She rested a sketchbook on her knee, licked the end of her pencil and began to draw.

"Thank you for staying so still…"

As she outlined the plant's long thick stem with broad strokes, the bird, startled by the appearance of a round piece of glass with an enlarged green eye behind it, flew away to find another flower. The girl ran her finger along the edge of the trumpet, delighting in the cool, velvety feel of it. Then she peered inside the top to see the nectar the hummingbird had been drinking from.

"That is so clever, like a perfect little jug. I wonder what it tastes like. Maybe I'll try a little, would you mind?" She lifted her finger, ready to dip it into the flower, and at that moment an angry cry rumbled through the understory of the rainforest, making her drop her pencil.

"Fern!"

Hastily she pushed her sketchbook back into her bag and set off at a run through the tangled, twisted undergrowth.

"Sorry, Dad," she panted. "I was looking at this *amazing* flower. You should have seen the colour." She thrust her sketchbook under his nose and he looked at her drawing. His disapproval was evident in the way he curled up the outer edges of his nostrils.

"What is its Latin name, Fern?"

"Um … is it an orchid?" she said.

"No, Fern, it is a *Heliconia rostrata*. A lobster claw heliconia. What is its family?"

"Prawns?" she giggled.

Darwin Featherstone shook his head. "The *Heliconia* plant is part of the *Heliconiaceae* family. You should know how to identify these simple plants by now." He turned away and peered into the rainforest ahead. "We must hurry. I want day camp set up by twelve hundred hours so that your mother and I have the whole afternoon to hunt. Sunset is at nineteen hundred hours and we have a long list of plants to find before then."

Her dad set off again, poking his walking stick into the forest floor as he went to check there was nothing lurking in the thick carpet of rainforest.

"These boots are so heavy," said Fern as she half-ran to keep up. "I'm sure they're giving me blisters. Why can't I take them off?"

"You can't walk through the Amazon Rainforest barefoot, Fern, we might have another *incident*," said her mum, who had been waiting for them patiently. Defina had grown up in the lush green mountains of the South Island of New Zealand and was a taller version of Fern, with the same cloud of red hair, but without Fern's constellation of freckles that she'd inherited from her Scottish dad.

9

"But we've been walking since we woke up."

"And we will walk some more," her dad called back. "Keep your eyes peeled for Brazilian wandering spiders – they don't make webs, they walk along the floor. You wouldn't want to meet one of those, I can tell you, even with your boots on."

As the sun hit its highest point in the sky, her dad stopped. He looked left, then right, he looked behind and in front, and then he heaved down the heavy wooden trunk he was carrying.

"Flat ground, good visibility and partial shade," he said. "The perfect spot for our day camp. Let's unload."

First they unpacked microscopes for studying stamens, stigmas and anthers – small portable ones that could be whipped out to look at a plant where it grew. Then there were the weather instruments: barometers and rain gauges for making sure they were not caught out by a tropical storm. The Featherstone family had worked in some of the most extreme environments of the world, hunting out rare plants for medical research, and the weather was often fierce.

"Can I come today?" asked Fern. "I'll be very good. I won't drop anything, or dig up the wrong plant."

"You have studies to do." Her dad kept his eyes focused on what he was doing.

"I could do it ever so quickly and then come and

help you? I promise I won't cut off the flowers to make a necklace this time."

"How will you become a great plant hunter yourself if you don't dedicate time to your lessons? Learn first, field work later." He pulled on a pair of thick leather gloves to protect his hands, and Fern handed him a small pack which he hoisted onto his shoulder. Then she moved over to her mum and stood hopefully by her side.

"Can I come with *you*, Mum?"

Defina pulled out a box of soil sample jars and put one in her plant-hunting bag.

"You must do as your father says, Fern-bug," she said in her soft lilting voice.

"I'll be very quiet, I promise. I won't sing or talk to the plants or do *anything* to distract you."

Fern's mum settled a kiss on her cheek. "Not today." She glanced down at the compass that hung around her neck and followed her husband into the deeper rainforest.

Fern sat in the middle of their day camp with a sigh and took her books from her bag.

"Why would anyone ever want to spend even a second of their day learning Latin?" She made a face, though she was the only person who might have seen it. "It's a language as dead as a dodo bird, or should

I say, *Raphus cucullatus*, and that is as dead as dead can be. Extinct, even!" She chuckled at her own joke.

Fern picked up her Latin book and bent her head over the pictures, trying to will her brain to behave. But very quickly a familiar tingling feeling started in her fingers and toes, then moved towards the centre of her, refusing to go away.

Unable to ignore the call of curiosity for a second longer, Fern stood up. She could just glimpse her parents hard at work through the veil of green undergrowth. She knew they would be there for several hours. So she put her old desert hat on her head and set off to explore the rainforest herself.

CHAPTER TWO

Fern knew things about plants that she hadn't learned from her dreaded textbooks. She knew that when plants were scared they could not run away like an animal could, but that some could shoot chemicals that smelled horrible to chase away predators. She had learned the hard way that others had nasty prickles or poisonous pollen, and she stayed away from those. When she cut herself she knew which plants healed, and when she stung herself she knew which plants soothed. Best of all, she knew which plants she could climb.

Seeing a rubber tree, she flung off her hateful boots, then slotted her grubby fingers and toes into the nooks of the trunk and quickly shimmied up it. While children in classrooms across the world studied how the Amazon River wiggled its way across a coloured map, Fern's geography lesson that day consisted of sitting in the treetop chewing on a melting chocolate bar she had discovered in her pocket, and spying on the sluggish, brownish, dullish Amazon River below.

There was a rustling in a nearby tree and a small face appeared between the leaves. It considered Fern for a moment, and then the monkey decided that she was no threat and joined her in making itself a small den. It was peaceful up here with just the monkey for company and Fern could see for miles and miles.

She followed the course of the river until her eye caught sight of a muddle of green spanning it like a line of emerald stepping stones. Feeling the tingle of curiosity again, and having left her binoculars behind at day camp, Fern decided she would just have the *smallest* peek at what was on the river, and then, she promised out loud, she would get straight back to her Latin verbs.

"Thank you for having me!" she said to the rubber tree and slid down its trunk.

The green stretching across the great river turned out to be a line of enormous lily pads. "What magnificent things you are. Like giant tea saucers with frilly purple edges. I wonder... I wonder if you could hold my weight? You certainly look strong enough. Perhaps I'll try stepping on the first of you and see."

Gently, Fern eased herself onto the enormous flat leaf. It didn't even dent! She bounced a couple of times, laughing at the feeling – it was like being on a floating trampoline. Feeling brave, she crept onto the next pad, and the next, and before she knew it, she was halfway across the river and could hardly see the bank she had started out from.

Finding the perfect pad on which to sit cross-legged and rest for a while, she watched dragonflies hover over the water like colourful helicopters. She was as hot as a hair dryer away from the cover of the trees, so she dangled her toes in the river for a moment, knowing that leaving them in too long might lead to them becoming a snack for a passing golden-flecked piranha fish.

A strange clicking noise made her jump. She turned and saw the black flash of a shiny shelled pollinating beetle hovering over one of the lily pads. "Don't land," she shouted at it. "You'll regret it!"

But it was too late. The beetle landed on the open flower of the lily and as Fern watched the flower closed its silken prison gates around it. She knew that the lily would hold it there for a whole day before releasing the insect to spread its pollen.

She leaned forward to listen to the worried rattle of the trapped beetle.

"Why do you hold onto them for so long?" Fern asked the plant. "Surely it could get the pollen quickly and you could let it go again? The poor thing sounds like it might have a heart attack, it's so scared."

Standing up quickly to see if she could help the beetle in any way, the lily pad seemed to tip in annoyance and she lost her balance and toppled forward into the cold water.

"Help," she gargled. "Hel—"

The 'p' was lost when she swallowed a whole cupful of smelly river water.

Moving from country to country every few weeks as her family had, Fern had never really learned to swim beyond a basic doggy paddle. As she started to sink, the long stems of the lily became wrapped around her legs and she struggled to kick.

With sudden clarity she could see she must be moments from running out of air – and that it was her own silly fault – but then her feet brushed the bottom and she managed to push off from the silty riverbed and break free of the lily stems. She popped up through the surface, gasping the fresh air gratefully and clinging to the edge of one of the pads.

The relief did not last long once she saw the eyeball. It was about two metres away, and looking straight at her. Fern didn't know as much about animals as she did about plants, but she was fairly sure that the eyeball, and the bubble-blowing nostril that now appeared next to it, belonged to a black caiman, a type of fearsome Amazonian crocodile that wasn't usually fussy about what was on the menu.

A second eye appeared, flecked with gold, and the caiman watched her unblinkingly, as if deciding whether she was worth the effort. Then, ever so slowly, it began to glide through the water towards her.

A scream rose in Fern's throat, but she knew there was no one near enough to hear. Instead, fear gave her the kick she needed and she managed to grab onto the next lily pad and pull herself out of the water. But the caiman rose from the river like a scaly rocket and launched itself forward – it wasn't going to give up that easily on a tasty-looking piece of lunch.

Fern flung herself desperately from one lily pad to another, hearing splashes behind her as the caiman rose again. Reaching the final lily pad, she rolled herself onto the shore just as the clatter of its giant jaws closed on thin air. Turning, she saw the creature's prehistoric head was so close that she could have reached out and touched it. But now she was on the riverbank, the caiman sank into the water again and disappeared silkily into the depths.

Fern lay for a moment looking up at the clouds spinning in the sky. Then she sat and funnelled the water out of her ears. Finding a long stick, she managed to fish her floating hat from the river and put it back on her damp, matted hair. She nodded in gratitude to the lily pads, and was about to turn towards the camp when a long shadow fell over her.

CHAPTER THREE

Darwin Featherstone's face was particularly fearsome when he had been disobeyed. His craggy nose and angled chin seemed sharper and his eyes spoke on behalf of his mouth, which stayed firmly shut – for now, at least.

"I didn't mean to go in the river, I really didn't, Dad," Fern spluttered. "The lily pads are just so *giant* and I wanted a little look at them and I was telling one of them off for trapping a poor wee beetle and then... Well, I think it was cross with me and I fell in." A tiny frog jumped out of the pocket of her drenched dungarees and hopped away as if it knew what was coming.

"How dare you disobey me?" her dad said. Fern gulped like an Amazon fish. "You know you should not leave day camp and you know that you must never go near water without us. Do you not listen to me, Fern?"

She shrugged damply.

"I will not have this nonsense again. Plants can't understand you, Fern." He turned around and began

walking back to their camp. Stumbling to her feet, Fern ran after him.

"But what if they could? Imagine if they *could*, Dad. We don't know that they can't. Not for sure."

"Fern, stop it. You have swallowed too much river water. Plants and humans cannot communicate and never will."

"The other Darwin thought that they could hear things," Fern said defiantly. "You told me that Charles Darwin made his son play bassoon to plants as an experiment. If they can hear things maybe they *can* understand us."

Reaching camp, her dad searched through his trunk and covered the orchid he had found with a hessian sack. The plant was used to the cooler temperatures of the canopy floor and Fern stepped forward to help him.

"Charles Darwin was right about many things, but nobody is right about everything. Focus on what fascinating things plants *can* do, not on what they cannot. It is no good making up fairy tales about them." With that, her dad strode angrily back into the thick of the rainforest, leaving Fern staring helplessly after him.

"Leave him be. He needs to cool off. You gave him a fright. You're his only daughter and he loves you very much."

Defina kneeled beside her and helped Fern out of her dungarees, then plucked something cressy from her sodden matt of hair. Fern didn't feel very loved. Surely if someone loved you they never told you off like Dad did when he was cross. Her mum tapped her on the end of her nose lightly with her finger and then stood up.

"I have heard you chatting to the plants, Fern-bug. It's very sweet but they can't actually understand you, you must know that. Don't make your dad cross again, he has so much important work to do."

Later that evening, Fern's parents sat around a flickering fire that shot orange sparks into the dark Amazon sky like shoals of goldfish. Occasionally a bat would dive-bomb them and then disappear, screeching into the night. Fern, who had sensed that one of her parents' "talks" was brewing in the way that weather watchers know a storm is coming, was listening from inside their family tent, which was snuggled among the roots of a Kapok tree.

"I'm anxious about Fern," said her mum, sipping sweet tea from a coconut bowl.

"Again?" said her dad, but not unkindly.

"This time I am *really* worried. What happened today – it's happening more and more. Fern's imagination leads her to dangerous places. This strange life of ours was fine when she was a baby but she is older now. She needs … *more*."

Fern, who was tracing the shadow pattern of the branches on the roof of the tent, wanted to shout that she didn't need anything more, that she liked their life just fine, thank you very much. But then they would have known she was listening – so instead she let out a small pretend snore.

Her dad was quiet for a moment. Fern peeked out and saw his face in the firelight, criss-crossed with shadows.

"I agree she is an overly curious child."

"I thought that children were *supposed* to be curious?" Defina's voice had an edge. Inside her sleeping bag, Fern nodded her strong agreement.

"She must learn to curb her curiosity and dedicate herself to her studies. She has such potential, but she seems to think plants are just for having fun. Her plant identification skills are sporadic, and her grasp of Latin is weak. If she wants to become a botanist and a plant hunter, she must start concentrating *now*. There is no time to waste."

"Have you thought that being a botanist might not be what she wants?"

Darwin looked at her as if she had gone mad.

"You didn't become what *your* father wanted you to," she chided him. "He dreamed of you being in the army, like him."

"That was different," he said. "After my mother died there was only one career I could ever have chosen: exploring the unknown plants of the world to develop medicines, to help cure terrible diseases. My path was set at her graveside." Fern heard a deep sorrow in her dad's voice and wanted to fling herself from her sleeping bag and give him one of her special hugs.

Her mum waited a beat, gathering her knees towards her and hugging them tightly to her chest.

"She's just a little girl. This isn't the life for her, there is other learning she needs to do."

"She *is* learning," said her dad stubbornly. "At least she would be, if she could be bothered." Fern had to clamp her lips together to stop her from telling her dad that the only people who could be bothered with learning Latin needed their heads examined.

"Learning from books is not the same as learning about people, and she's doing very little of either, dear husband." Fern saw her mum lay a hand on her dad's. "Our daughter has reached the age of ten and she has never had a friend. We are never anywhere for more than a few weeks or a month at a time. When I was her age, I had brothers and sisters and cousins and a whole community. And you – well, you had that unusual brother of yours to rub off your edges."

She smiled fondly at her husband and carried on. "I think Fern is lonely. She has no friends and so she thinks the plants can keep her company. I… I sometimes think it would be better for her if we sent her away from us." Fern felt every part of her body freeze icicle-hard. There was a long silence as her parents stared deep into the fire, as if it might hold the answers they needed.

Fern felt a bolt of fury. How could her parents even *think* such a thing? They couldn't really send her away, could they? They wouldn't. Would they?

That night, as the fire burned itself out, watched by her silent parents, Fern made a whispered vow to herself. "I will work hard at my Latin *and* my plant studies. I will wear my boots, I will not go exploring on my own and I will never, never, talk to plants, not ever again."

CHAPTER FOUR

Inside the very same tent, several days later, Fern was packing her things into an old, worn suitcase. She chose a few of her most precious treasures – a pine cone she had collected in a Californian forest that was as big as her head, a leaf skeleton from a maple tree in Canada, and her pride and joy, a pacay pod from Peru that made a noise like rainfall when you shook it. The rest of her seed collection she would have to leave behind – there were so many of them that they could have filled the entire suitcase. She slipped outside and buried her Latin book under a pile of rocks for the Amazonian mini beasts to munch on. If she really did have to go, then that hateful book was not coming with her.

Fern looked at her desert hat perched on the crown of the tent. She wouldn't need it where she was going and yet she couldn't bear to leave it behind, and so she placed it on top of her other things, like a rather battered-looking cherry on a cake.

It took all of Fern's courage (and plenty of muscle strength) to close the bulging suitcase. She fingered the airline labels that were tied to its handle with string; crumpled paper memories of all the magical corners of the world they had been to as a family, and she felt something large and lump-like form at the back of her throat.

Once her suitcase was ready, she fastened her arms to the trunk of the Kapok tree that had stood over their camp like a protective umbrella these last months. It was a little like trying to hug a dinosaur.

"Thank you," she whispered into the bark. The tree rustled its leaves slightly, as if saying it would miss her too. All there was to suggest that they had lived there for so many weeks was a flattened circle where the family tent had been. The Featherstones had left a trail of circles like this one, like a dot-to-dot across a map of the world. But this was to be her last dot, then her parents would carry on dotting without her. She turned her back on the circle and walked away, squeezing her insides tight.

Later, at the airport, her dad handed Fern her plant-hunting bag. Inside were her binoculars, her magnifying glass and her sketchbook.

"I don't think I'll need it in a city," she said quietly.

"Cities aren't so different to jungles when you

scratch beneath the surface," he said. "Your tools might come in useful." And he looped it onto her sagging shoulders. "Once our Amazonian specimens have been packaged to send to the laboratories we will be leaving for the Democratic Republic of the Congo. There won't be any phone signal there and we will not be able to get a letter to you for some time, but you must not worry about us."

Fern's chin fell to her chest and she couldn't lift it up again.

Defina looked down at her daughter's face as if she was trying to memorize every part of it. Words seemed to have deserted her, so Darwin took Fern by the hand and led her briskly to an air hostess who would look after her on the journey. Then he returned to his wife, linked his arm through hers, and they walked away. Neither of them dared to look back.

Most air hostesses you meet are kindly. They smell sweet and do their best to make sure that your journey is a pleasant one. But not Miss Bay. She had bunions the size of golf balls from standing on her feet for so many hours and her smile curled downwards rather than upwards. "This way," she said roughly, prodding Fern in the direction the plane with one of her bumpy crimson nails.

On the runway, a woman was pointing at a collection of wooden crates strewn across the blazing tarmac.

"I will not have my collection out of my sight." A large straw hat was perched on the woman's head and she wore a white linen travel suit with a thick leather belt around her slim waist. "It will have to come on board with me. All of it." She waved the champagne glass in her hand and Fern was curious to see that it wasn't filled with an amber bubbly drink but with a bright green one. A single ice cube floated inside.

"There is no room, madam," said the plane's captain. Fern wondered what was in the crates. Maybe poisonous snakes or rainforest lizards?

"Then you will have to leave someone behind," said the straw-hatted woman, smiling graciously and handing the captain her empty glass. Not waiting for an answer, she began to climb the metal stairs at the front of the plane, the skirt of her suit swishing about her legs. She paused halfway up and, without turning around, she clicked her fingers at a short assistant, as wide as he was tall, who was waiting below. He picked up the first crate and followed her, very slowly, up the stairs. Dressed as he was in a thick three-piece tweed suit, the buttons of his waistcoat hardly holding over his taut chest, sweat was dripping down his face.

Fern turned and climbed the stairs at the back of the plane, forcing her feet to do what her heart did not want to. Reaching the top, she paused and looked back once more at the Amazon. The sun was setting, exploding colours across the sky like upset tins of paint – pink, orange, red and yellow. Beyond the runway, she could see the back of her parents' car as it disappeared into the sunset, leaving a trail of golden dust in the air behind it.

Her heart had pins and needles as the doors of the plane shut and it careered down the runway, launching itself in the direction of her new life.

"You have everything you need," Miss Bay growled at Fern once the seat belt light went off. It was a statement rather than a question.

"Could I have some water, please?" said Fern.

"Greedy child," she growled, shoving a glass in Fern's direction. "Put your shoes back on or you'll stink the whole plane out." With that she clumped away down the aisle.

Fern drank the water and leaned forward to try and catch glimpses of the ocean outside the window as the plane dipped and rose like a swallow returning home. When her neighbour began to snore, a familiar restless jiggling feeling started inside her, and she unbuckled her seat belt and climbed out into the aisle.

Being extremely sad didn't appear to have banished her curiosity.

Reaching the front of the plane, she peered through the curtain that divided First Class from the rest of the passengers. Here too there was a medley of snores. The crates she had seen on the runway were lined up in the aisles. Standing guard over them was the lady's assistant.

As Fern watched, an alarm went off in his pocket and he bent and picked up a glass bottle, pressing a nozzle on the top of it and unleashing a shower of dark droplets over the crates. A dank smell navigated her nostrils and made her want to sneeze.

Once he'd finished, the assistant sat down again, taking out a book – but before he had even turned a page his head fell back, the book crumpled on his lap and his own grunting snore joined the others.

Crouching on her hands and knees, Fern crept through the curtain and along the aisle, stopping by the first crate. Putting an eye next to one of the gaps in the wood, she blinked in surprise. There were not animals inside, like she had expected, but plants! Several rows of them, packed tightly, their leaves and stems twisted together. "You poor things," she whispered. "You look so miserable in there. I wonder where you are going?"

There was a jolt as the plane hit a cumulus cloud and lurched downwards. The movement forced one of the crates open, and something was tossed out of it. It rolled quickly down the aisle, sprinkling compost as it turned, stopping at Fern's knees. The plane bounced up again, clearing the cumulus, and the plant rolled up Fern's knees and onto her lap. The crate lid shut as if nothing had happened.

Looking around to check that nobody was watching, Fern picked up the pot. Inside was a small plant, hardly taller than her little finger. It had two spindly tendrils growing out of it, like miniature green laces. There was a nodule on each side that looked like coiled leaves and on top of the plant was a tiny pod, no bigger than a pea. Poking up from the pod was a single downy spear, as soft as the hair on a baby's head.

"Well, aren't you the oddest-looking thing ever?" she whispered. "I think you're just a baby, aren't you?"

To her enormous surprise, the plant curled one of its thin tendrils around her finger and nodded its pod. It was almost as if the plant had understood what she had said.

CHAPTER FIVE

At that moment there was a noise a truffle pig would have been proud of; the assistant sprung awake at the sound of his own snore and sat up, eyes blinking in surprise. Fern leaned back, disappearing from his view.

"Anything could have happened!" he said to himself, shaking his head crossly. "Falling asleep on such an important job would be a sackable offence. You are not good enough, Ginkgo. She'll realize that soon enough, and you will be back where you belong: in the gutter."

He was so near to where Fern was nestled in the aisle that she could smell his slightly sour breath and see every heather-coloured thread woven through his green waistcoat.

A loud thumping noise came from behind Fern, and she turned to see Miss Bay's clumpy feet heading in her direction. Tucking the plant inside the front

pocket of her dungarees, Fern slithered into the space below an empty seat. She waited until the hostess had passed and then slipped out of the First-Class cabin. Back in her seat it took only a second to tuck herself under a blanket and pretend to be asleep.

"Little blighter, I'm sure she wasn't here when I last looked," said Miss Bay, marching back down the aisle towards her. "Blimmin' Houdinis, these children are. As if I haven't got enough work on my hands making that green juice muck for Lady Rich. Who does she think she is, the Queen?"

When she had gone, Fern opened her eyes and patted her pocket to check the baby plant hadn't fallen out.

"Are you all right down there?" she whispered, and it nodded in reply. Would it be *very* wrong of her to keep it? Mum and Dad had taught her it was wrong to steal, of course, but there had been so many plants in the crates, would such a little one as this even be missed?

After all, this was the moment she had been waiting for her whole life! She had been practising for so many years and now, finally, a plant understood her. There might not be any plants in London, she didn't want to give this one up just when she had mastered plant-speak. If only her dad had been here, she could have shown him that she had been right all along: plants could understand people, you only had to speak to them the right way!

With thoughts of her dad came a fresh wave of sadness, but somehow Fern felt less alone knowing that the little plant was with her. As though it understood how she was feeling, a tendril wormed its way out of her pocket and patted her gently on the chin. This made up Fern's mind.

"You can come with me. We're going to London, a great big city where neither of us belong, but I won't be staying long – I'll be back with my family before you know it. And you can come with me."

Fern didn't realize she'd fallen asleep until she was woken by a sharp rap on her head. Miss Bay was staring down at her angrily. "Wake up, lazybones. Didn't I tell you to put your shoes back on? We'll be landing soon and then you're on your own."

As the plane bounced through plump clouds and glided into the gentle grey skies below, a tannoy crackled to life. "Good afternoon, this is your captain speaking. The crew and myself hope you have enjoyed your journey with us. If you look out of your window you will see that the weather is wet in London today but as we start our descent, please sit back, relax and take this opportunity to look beyond the drizzle and see the great city in all its glory."

Fern pushed her nose against the cold circle of a window, rain pattering on the thick glass, as they passed over endless rows of tiny square houses and roads jammed with miniature cars. She wondered how a girl like her was ever going to survive in a place like this. She wiggled her toes nervously.

A river looped through the heart of the city, sluggish and steely. From the corner of her eye, she saw a flash of green. She pushed as close as she could against the window until her nose folded over.

There was a green line across the river! It looked like the line of giant lily pads that had been the start of all of this mess, only – and this bit surprised her – they were even *bigger*. She sat back with a surprised *thud*. London didn't seem like the kind of place where giant Amazonian lilies would grow!

"Did you see that?" she said to the man sitting next to her, but he was wearing ear plugs and carried on sleeping. She reached for her boots and shoved her reluctant feet into them.

As the plane swooped towards the runway like an eager metal duck, there was a short, sharp jerk and it leaped quickly back into the air. The tannoy screeched to life again and the captain spoke. "I'm sorry for the scare," she said. "We have been instructed to circle a few more times before landing. There appears to be a covering of moss over the entire runway. I've never seen anything like it."

CHAPTER SIX

When the plane finally came to an uneasy landing, Fern followed Miss Bay into the bowels of the enormous airport and found her old suitcase bobbing along the conveyor belt; she scooped it off and hugged it like a long-lost friend. They walked into a room below a sign that said *Nothing to Declare*, and Fern felt her heart quicken. She did have something to declare. She was carrying a stolen item. What might the police do with a plant thief?

Ahead, the white-suited lady was talking to a customs official, the plant crates piled high on a trolley beside her.

"No, you cannot check my specimens, I am afraid. It has been a long flight and they are extremely sensitive. I am a very important botanist." The nervous face of the customs man was reflected in the lenses of her oversized sunglasses.

"Do you have permits for those plants?" he said.

The woman took a raft of papers from a sleek briefcase, but before he had a chance to see them, she whipped them away again. Without another word, she glided out of the customs room, followed by her assistant pushing the trolley. Fern saw that there were words stencilled on the wood of the crates in grey paint: *The Magnolia Hotel*.

"Your parents said you would be picked up from here." Miss Bay pushed Fern and her little suitcase out of the main door of the airport into the dim light and cold cuddle of London, and was gone without a backwards glance. Lines of passengers were swarming towards a collection of beetle-black taxis waiting with their engines running. Fern followed, feeling in her pocket for the piece of paper on which her dad had written an address:

Mr Edward Featherstone,
67 Dandelion Road,
London

Something tapped against her hip, startling Fern out of her worry. Turning to look, she saw that it was a hat, spinning around and around in the wet wind. As it began to lower towards a waiting puddle, she pounced and caught it just in time.

"You have something of mine, I believe." She turned and saw the botanist, bare-headed now but for a thin calico scarf. As the woman lifted her sunglasses, Fern saw her eyes for the first time: the vivid green of ivy leaves. Did the botanist know about the baby plant nestled inside her dungarees pocket? She could feel it squirming, as if it was worried about something.

"My hat. You have my hat."

Relief flowed through Fern. She handed the hat over, feeling the brush of the botanist's hand against her own.

"Thank you," she said, stroking it a couple of times before putting it back on her calico-swaddled head. "It is my favourite, I would have quite hated for it to be ruined." And then she was gone, sliding into the front seat of a waiting van, leaving her assistant to load the crates into the boot.

Fern looked after her thoughtfully. Who would have thought that a botanist could be so glamorous and beautiful? Her parents and their plant-loving friends always looked like they had been dragged through a bush backwards (which, more often than not, they had) but the lady botanist looked like a film star. Fern couldn't help but admire her.

The taxi that pulled up next looked like all the other ones, apart from the sign in the window with

Fern's name written on it in swirling, messy writing. She let out a sigh of relief – she wouldn't have to find her own way across this jungle. Taking a deep breath and wedging her own hat on her head, which felt welcomingly familiar, Fern climbed into the back seat.

A sweet smell greeted her and she saw that behind the wheel sat a large lady in a printed dress, her long black hair dotted with fresh sweet peas.

"Greetings, Fern Featherstone!" she said. Her face turned up in all the right places and made Fern feel a little more cheerful. "You look *just* how he described you. Are you ready to go to Dandelion Road, missy?"

Fern nodded, her heart being pelted with little darts of nerves.

"You leave it with ol' Blossom. I know London better than most people know their fingers and toes. You just sit back and enjoy the ride. Welcome to the greatest city in the world."

Fern nestled her nose against the window and watched as the city grew bigger and bigger, as if someone was modelling it from larger and larger pieces of clay. There were penguin-like huddles of people at each traffic light, motorbikes bending in and out of double-decker buses, old-fashioned buildings and shops strung with fairy lights. Her eyes hardly knew where to look, there was so much to see.

"Ned keeps me on speed dial – I drive him everywhere. He's never bothered to learn, you see. Truth is, I can't imagine him behind the wheel; he can hardly put one foot in front of the other in a straight line," she chuckled. "Do you know I'd never been to so many libraries before I started driving him – only my local – but now I could take you to any one in the whole of London. Hundreds of them, there are! Makes me think, how many books are there in the whole of the city?"

She was interrupted at that moment by a cannon ball crash on the roof of the taxi. Fern jumped upright in the seat in surprise.

"What was that?"

"Don't worry, we just passed under the Chelsea coconut grove."

"A coconut grove? In a city?"

"You heard me right! No one knows where the trees came from, they just arrived one day, fully grown. I got dents all over the taxi from coconut bombs." She hooted with laughter, slapping the steering wheel. "There's talk of some chappy called the Guerrilla Gardener planting it all, but no one seems to be able to catch him at it."

Fern thought this city was getting stranger and stranger. Why were gorillas doing gardening?

They tunnelled on and on through the city, finally leaving the tall part of London behind, and turning east. Here the buildings were smaller, as if they had been given shrinking powder: rows and rows of higgledy-piggledy houses. They turned into a quiet road and Blossom turned off the engine.

"There now, you must be happy to be at the end of your long journey!"

"It feels more like the beginning," Fern said nervously, stepping out onto the pavement. She touched her hand to her dungarees pocket, making sure her new friend was still there.

"Well, good luck, Miss Fern," Blossom said, sticking her head out of the window. "I'm sure we'll meet again." She steered the taxi back into the road and drove away.

Fern found number sixty-seven and opened the front gate. Until that point her uncle had just been a name on a piece of paper, but now he felt tremendously, terrifyingly real.

CHAPTER SEVEN

It felt like a very long minute before Fern heard a small scuffling behind the door, and then the sharp sound of metal on metal as a latch was turned. She hugged herself nervously.

The man who appeared from behind the door, however, looked quite the opposite of scary. He was grasshopper-thin and wore clothes that were a little large for him: a mottled brown jacket hung limply off his shoulders, shadowing a baggy jumper underneath, and his trousers were worn at the knees. On his nose perched a pair of small round glasses, and his eyebrows were remarkable for their bushiness – like shaggy caterpillars on the verge of becoming a chrysalis.

He seemed surprised to find a rather messy-looking child on his doorstep, but he cleared his throat and said, "You must be Fern. At least, I presume you are, as I only usually have children calling here at Halloween. But as it is August and not October, and you are not dressed as a polyester pumpkin, you had better come in."

His mouth broke into a cautious smile and Fern's heart rate eased to a gentle pitter patter.

Beyond the door was a small, cramped hall. She put down her suitcase and sat on top of it to take off her shoes and socks, before wriggling her toes about gratefully.

"You might want to keep those on, actually," he said. "I am afraid my floors are not very clean. I have little time or skill for domestic matters."

"Oh, I don't like shoes much," Fern said. "I've never really worn them, so if it's all right with you, Mr Featherstone, I will keep them off."

"Very well, of course. This is your home now, and if you don't want to wear shoes, then you do not need to. However, you must not call me Mr Featherstone, that I insist on. I am your Uncle Ned." He held out his hand and she put hers inside it. It was cold and soft, with fingers so long and spindly they felt like they would be most at home playing a grand piano.

Fern looked around curiously at this place he had called her new home. There was a small table piled high with unopened letters, next to which waited a pair of old leather gloves. The hat stand was so cluttered with coats and scarves that it leaned like the Tower of Pisa, looking like it might topple over and smother the floor with wool and felt at any moment. And below, on the knobbly floorboards, were stacks of paper of various heights, each tied up in a bow of brown string. Fern had spent very little time in houses in her short life but this one, she thought, felt friendly.

"I am a writer," Uncle Ned said, by way of apologizing for the mess. "I am afraid I spend most of my days sleeping and my nights writing. I do admit that I have been wondering if I shall be any good to you as an uncle since I have no previous experience in the role – and we have never actually met before today." His glasses slipped anxiously down his isosceles-shaped nose and he pushed them back up again.

"What do you write?" asked Fern, who had never met a writer before.

"Medieval fiction!" he said, his eyebrows springing above his glasses. "Battles and blood, mostly. Lots of bludgeoning and beheading. My ancestor – and yours, of course – was a famous knight. Edward De Valburt Linneas Featherstone. You might have heard of him? No? Ah, well. That was his."

Following his finger, Fern saw a shiny suit of armour standing proudly behind the hat stand. Above the suit, hanging from a nail, was a chunky sword. It looked like it might still have a smidgen of blood on it, and perhaps a hair or two. Fern's mouth popped open and she had to force it shut again. "The hero of my books, Garridan, has become rather a good friend of mine."

He looked so sincere that Fern didn't let herself laugh, though she wanted to. No wonder her mum had said he was unusual – he seemed to think his story was real!

"Now, are you hungry?" Uncle Ned asked. "Do they feed people on planes? I spend so much time writing that I never really leave London. Quite unlike your own parents, who cannot seem to stand still for more than five minutes."

Fern's tummy had been telling her for some time that it was hungry, so she followed him through a low doorway into the kitchen. Every surface here was covered in papers – there were even papers stuck to the walls and a couple tacked to the windows.

"This is both kitchen and office, I'm afraid. My memory is a leaky sieve so I have to write ideas down as soon as they come to me." He rapped at his head with his thin knuckles. "Now," he looked at Fern and smiled, "tea and toast, I think. I'm not much of a cook but I am very good at toast. My speciality, you might say. The toast must be hot, it must be buttered, but after that, the possibilities are quite endless." His eyes gleamed with excitement behind his glasses.

He flitted around the kitchen, cutting a thick chunk of bread from a crusty loaf and inserting it into a toaster, and then putting an old battered kettle on a hob.

"You are a little older than I expected – time does fly so, doesn't it? Especially when you spend most of your time with words and not people, like I do. I cannot quite believe you are nearly as tall as me." He took a photograph from the wall and handed it to her. "This was sent to me by your parents when you were born. Alaska, I believe, chasing after one of those elusive undiscovered plants they always seem to be on the trail of."

Fern took the photograph from him and saw a grainy image of her parents. Her mum was holding what looked like a handful of blankets but was, on closer inspection, a tiny baby. She gulped, thinking it would be extremely rude to cry when they had only just met, but she couldn't make the feeling disappear. It simmered around her chest somewhere, waiting for a chance to pounce.

"I think you will need to go to school," Uncle Ned said, putting a cup of grey liquid in front of her. "There's one at the end of the road that should do." Fern felt her heart speed up a bit. *School*. She had watched children all over the world on their way to school in the mornings, and she had made up stories in her head about what might happen when they got there, but she had never actually been inside one.

"However," Uncle Ned continued, "it appears that it is the summer holidays, so that won't be possible for some weeks. I am afraid until then you will have to amuse yourself."

They sat at an old pine table and ate a piece of toast smothered in creamy, salted butter. Uncle Ned put something called marmalade on his, but Fern decided not to as it looked a little like worms swimming in orange slime. They chewed in companionable silence.

"Do you have a garden?" she asked after a little while. On her ninth birthday, her parents had given her a copy of *The Secret Garden* and she had stayed up late into the night reading about Dickon and Mary and Colin. Entwined among the sadness of leaving her parents, there had been the tiniest trickle of hope that her uncle's garden would be like the one at Misselthwaite Manor: a proper English garden with roses and robins.

Uncle Ned pointed at the window. Through the pages that were stuck to it, Fern could just make out a clump of overgrown grass with what looked like a small metal cannon stationed in the middle of it.

"I've never really managed to keep green things alive," said Uncle Ned. "Apart from that one, of course."

He pointed to a plant on the top of the fridge, with long thin leaves trailing down like streamers. "It was a gift from your parents many years ago when they left on their first assignment. They said that if I remembered to water it each day, I might remember to feed myself too. I can't remember what they said it was called. Some complicated Latin name."

"It's a spider plant," said Fern. "A very handsome one."

"Is it indeed?" said Uncle Ned. "Well, somehow I have not killed it, but I think I am better at dealing with dead things than living ones, that is perhaps why I write about the past. Although I hope that I can manage you, as you are very much alive." He laughed silently, rocking backwards and forwards in his chair, until there was a noise from the front door.

"Ah, my newspaper. Late again. Gets later every day." He got up to fetch it and Fern turned and looked at the spider plant.

"Hello, I'm Fern Featherstone," she said politely. The spider plant did nothing. "We're going to be living together for a bit, just until I get back to my parents," she said. "I hope we can be friends." Still the spider plant did nothing. It didn't seem to have understood her at all. Had she imagined what had happened on the plane? At that moment her uncle skipped back into the room with a newspaper rolled under his arm.

"As a plant lover, I think you'll be pleased to discover we have our own botanical wonders in London. Rather a lot of them just recently, actually."

He unrolled the newspaper, which she saw was called *The Grapevine*, and flattened it on the table. "This one appeared last night quite out of the blue, as if it had fallen from space. Come to think of it, it *is* a little alien-like, isn't it?" The photograph showed a large, fat plant with what looked like eight long arms sticking out in all directions.

"It says here that it is a *Welwitschia mirabilis* and look, there behind it – " he tapped his finger on a pointy looking building – "is the House of Commons. It must have been terribly difficult for the politicians to get to work this morning." His tremendous eyebrows met in the middle of his face in a bushy frown.

"There has been quite a spate of unusual plants appearing – nobody seems to know what they are or why they are growing here, and the experts say they are reaching sizes much larger than in the wild. Perhaps it is our endless London rain." He chuckled.

"Are all these plants from the gorilla? Blossom mentioned something about him…"

"Oh, yes! But it's 'guerrilla' – just another name for a sort of secret gardener, since no one has actually seen him do it. He must be a very strong gentleman, with all these plants being rather on the large side. But enough about him! Finish your toast and I will show you around."

CHAPTER EIGHT

Uncle Ned led Fern back to the hall and up a winding flight of steps to the top of the house.

"This will be yours," he said, opening the door. The room had a small window poking out from the eaves, on either side of which hung dark, mustard-coloured curtains. On the wall was a painting of a lady in a puffy dress whose eyes seemed to be watching them. In the middle of the room was an iron bed and beside it, a large cardboard box.

"Sorry about that, it's far too heavy to carry downstairs on my own, and Garridan is useless at helping with this sort of thing. It's full of old things I haven't been able to bring myself to throw away. Perhaps you could use the box as a bedside table until I manage to get it moved?" Fern nodded, and he lowered her suitcase gently onto the floor.

"I'm afraid it is now time for me to write. I am in the middle of a very trying chapter, and I dare not stay away from it too long. Garridan keeps doing things I don't want him to, and I can't seem to rein him in. He really is quite the scoundrel!"

"But he's not real, is he?" said Fern. "Garridan, I mean. Isn't he just a character?"

Uncle Ned's eyebrows popped up in surprise.

"He's real enough to me. We've written nearly twelve books together; I know him almost better than I know myself. Although I admit he feels rather more like an enemy than a friend at the moment." He adjusted his glasses which seemed to fall down whenever his face did anything apart from stay perfectly still.

As he turned to leave, he paused at the doorway and looked at her.

"No doubt this is a rather difficult time for you, and it is a rather surprising time for me, but we will make the best of things together, I am sure. We will muddle through."

Then he half-bowed and left the room, his footsteps disappearing down the stairs. Almost immediately there came the clatter of typing from the kitchen, frantic bursts of noise interspersed by long, thoughtful silences.

Alone, Fern took the small plant from her dungarees pocket and perched it on the windowsill. Its soft spear, which had been flattened in the hiding place, popped upright again.

"Here we go, this should be a good spot for you, right where I can see you." She looked nervously at the plant. Had it all just been a dream?

But to her delight the plant nodded its pod enthusiastically.

"I'm so sorry, it must have been a bit cramped there in my pocket, but I didn't want anyone to see that I had stolen you." It flung out its tendrils in a long stretch and then spun its pod around to face the window.

Fern busied herself finding her pine cone and her other treasures, trying to make the room look a bit less unfriendly.

"Uncle Ned seems nice, doesn't he?" she said as she worked. The plant nodded again.

"If I am going to keep you, then I think you need a name. Mine is Fern Flora Featherstone, by the way. Fern is my mum's favourite type of plant – she's from New Zealand, you see – and Flora is the Latin name for plants. My parents love Latin. And plants." She felt the empty feeling again as she talked about them. "Featherstone is our surname."

The plant cocked its pod as if it didn't understand.

"Surnames are … well, I suppose it's a way of classifying us humans into families. But what shall I call you? I don't know what kind of plant you are or what your Latin name is." She considered the funny looking plant but was no closer to knowing what it was. "I shall have to make one up!"

She opened her plant-hunting bag and took out her magnifying glass and examined the plant carefully. It really was the strangest thing, gangly and weedy looking, like it might blow over in the slightest puff of wind. Fern had seen some amazing plants, and this one was decidedly unimpressive. But it could understand her and that made it very...

"I've got it. You are perfectly unique, unlike anything I have ever seen before, so I am going to call you Special."

The little plant clapped its tendrils together in delight.

With that decided, Fern began to unpack her few clothes and the rest of her treasures. She pushed her suitcase under the bed and hung her desert hat on the bed post, but it still didn't feel anything like home.

"Good night, Special," she said and dropped a kiss on its little pod. It squirmed with pleasure.

She got into the bed but it felt too high and unfriendly, so she got out again, lay on the floor, pulled off the soft duvet and rolled herself up in it.

Fern waited and waited for sleep to come. Usually, she was lulled to sleep by the sound of the wind in the trees and the rustle of plants mixed with the gentle sound of her parents breathing next to her. But the noises she heard here were not familiar. Through the floorboards came the clattering of Uncle Ned's typewriter, as it if was fighting a battle with him, and from the attic above she could hear the scuttle of mice waking up under the roof tiles.

She gave up and opened the musty curtains, looking out into the dark night for something dear to her. At first she couldn't find it. Then a cloud passed and there it was: just a calligraphy curve in the sky. But even this tiny moon was enough to make her feel more at home, for it was the same moon she had seen in every place they had ever been, and she knew her parents were somewhere out there beneath the very same moon. Even though she was so far away from them, that thought made her feel a little better.

She yawned. Tomorrow she would come up with a plan of how she was going to get back to them. It didn't matter how dangerous the rainforests of the Democratic Republic of the Congo were – she couldn't stay in this strange city without them.

Fern clambered back into the duvet roll and closed her eyes, and finally sleep came, with Special watching over her from its spot on the windowsill.

CHAPTER NINE

In the morning there were more unfamiliar noises. Fern woke to the quiet purr of the milkman's electric float and the clink of bottles landing on front steps. Two pigeons clattered across the roof and there was the sound of a baby whimpering through her bedroom wall.

The horrible homesickness of the night before had put itself away for now, and been replaced by a gentle nudge of curiosity that made her jump out of bed and rummage for some clothes. Outside, it was still raining.

"I thought it was supposed to be summer," she said to Special, who was having a morning stretch. "I hope it's going to be warm enough for you here. You might be a tropical plant and not used to the cold."

Downstairs, Uncle Ned was asleep on his elbows on the kitchen table. He woke with a start, shaking his head as if trying to remember where he was and who she was.

"That rogue Garridan had me most out of sorts last night, he kept dashing off to try and fight a rather

nasty knight who he often ends up losing battles with. I had to keep hauling him out of trouble and it was quite exhausting, my fingers are red raw from typing."

His glasses had fallen from his face, and he picked them up and rubbed them a few times with his shirt-end before putting them back on.

"Rain again," he said, peering out at the garden. "It does seem to rain an awful lot these days, more than when your father and I were boys." He yawned. "Bedtime for me – I hope it isn't going to be too strange a life for you here with my odd routine."

"I'll be fine, I'll go and play outside. I think I saw a park from the taxi yesterday."

"Impossible, I am afraid. It is windy and wet and you'll catch a cold. I promised your parents I would look after you and, although I am no knight, I am honour-bound to keep my word. While it rains you must stay indoors. It's a perfect day to sit under a blanket and read; what more could one want than a day spent with words?"

He gathered his papers into a messy pile, tied a piece of string around them and went off to bed, a pen still stuck behind his ear.

Fern felt a bit deflated, but she couldn't disobey her uncle when they had only just met. So she decided she would explore indoors instead, starting with the large collection of books piled up along the downstairs and upstairs corridors, as well as on each step of the staircase. They were dusty, with pictures of medieval witches being dangled over lakes and men wearing things that looked like skirts and enormous wigs.

After a few hours of giggling at the strange pictures she began to feel very *inside-ish*, like a spring that needed to bounce but couldn't find anyone to set it off. She was a climby, exploringy, jumpy type of person and imprisoned inside a house, even a cosy one like this one, made her feel sluggish and out of sorts. It was like wearing shoes all over her body.

Thank goodness she had already decided that she was going to run away. Uncle Ned was so busy with his important book he probably wouldn't even notice.

She gave Special a kiss and then reached under the bed and pulled out her sketchbook. Sitting on the duvet on the floor, she flicked through her sketches of plants until she found a clean page. Across the top she wrote: *Fern Featherstone's Running-Away Plan.*

Then she put the end of the pencil in her mouth and sucked it thoughtfully. Although she had made up her mind to run away, she hadn't given any thought to *how*. But how hard could it be? People were always running away in stories. She just needed a place to start.

Her pencil hovered over the page as if it was waiting for her brain to give her an idea. But she was distracted by a buzzing above her – she looked up and saw a fly darting back and forth across cracks in the ceiling. It lowered its flight path towards the windowsill, where it stopped just short of her plant. There was a sudden flash of green and the buzzing stopped.

The fly had disappeared! Fern startled, her sketchbook falling off her lap.

"Special, did you do something to that fly? Where has it gone?" The plant bowed its pod coyly.

A suspicion passed through Fern's mind, but she needed proof – and that meant she needed another fly. There were plenty in the house; they had flown in to find refuge from the endless rain and then seemed to spend their whole time trying to find a way out again. She found one in the bathroom and, after a short battle, trapped it in a toothbrush mug and carried it into her bedroom.

"Sorry, little fly, but there is a small chance you might have to perish in the name of scientific investigation," she said before tipping it out of the mug and onto the windowsill. She stood back and waited and watched.

Nothing happened at first, and then, as the fly took off, Fern saw Special's tendrils start to shake. For a moment it did nothing, as if trying not to give in to an impulse, but then one tendril sprung out, and with a deft move, it patted the fly up towards its pod.

There was a hurried snap and the fly disappeared inside. A faint sound of buzzing came from the pod before it went eerily silent.

Fern stared at Special in astonishment.

"You ate that fly!" The plant nodded its pod, slightly guiltily.

"If you ate that fly, that must mean you are a carnivorous plant."

She pulled her plant-hunting bag out from under her bed, attached her magnifying glass to her eye and gave Special a thorough examination from bottom to top. When she leaned right into its pod she could just see a tiny slit that must have opened to catch the fly. Tapping it gently with her fingers made Special open it wide. Inside she saw hundreds of tiny hairs like miniature teeth.

"You aren't a Venus flytrap, I know what they look like and it's not like you. So what *are* you?"

She took up her notebook, turned the page over from her running-away plan, and began to scribble down pictures and words like she had seen her mum do when she was trying to identify a plant. After half an hour she threw it to one side in frustration.

"It's no good, I am the most useless botanist there ever was. Why didn't I concentrate more on my studies, Special? I can't tell a ponytail palm from a Zanzibar croton. I just can't work out what genus you might be a member of. No wonder Mum and Dad sent me away."

Suddenly the study of botany felt relevant in the way that it hadn't when she read her dad's books, and she wanted to know things she had never wanted to know before. She gave herself a little shake.

"No, I'm going to find out what kind of plant you are! Let's see what else you can do with those funny tendrils of yours." She fetched a marble she had seen when she was exploring. "Can you catch?"

She threw the marble at the plant and Special flung up its tendrils, but it couldn't quite reach. It overbalanced, toppled off the windowsill and landed with a crash and a splattering of soil on the floor.

Fern ran and scooped up the pot, spooning the soil back into it with her hands and patting it down. It was then that she noticed a small white rectangular tag nestled in the soil. She picked it out carefully and put it in the palm of her hand, seeing that it was like the tags her parents used to name plants. Turning it over, she brushed off some soil and made out some letters that became words: *The Magnolia Hotel*.

It took only a moment to remember where she had seen the words before; they had been written on the crates on the plane. Underneath them, in smaller letters, were four more words. She had to strain her eyes as the writing was so small. She took out her magnifying glass again: *Natura non facit saltum*.

"What does that mean, I wonder?" she asked Special. "It turns out Latin does matter, after all, sometimes…" She slumped down on her floor bed, feeling cross with herself all over again.

CHAPTER TEN

The next morning Fern found that Uncle Ned had left her some bread and jam, a glass of orange juice and a note scribbled on a torn-off corner of his manuscript. As she sat at the table to eat her breakfast, she couldn't work out what had changed since the night before, and then she realized: at last, the rain had stopped.

Garridan finally behaved himself last night and I managed to write one thousand words – that is nine hundred more than the night before! So I have gone to bed early to celebrate. Since the rain has stopped you will be perfectly safe exploring Dandelion Road, but don't go any further as there are rumours that more giant plants appeared overnight. Buy yourself some lunch from the bakery and don't forget your key – I got it cut specially. Enjoy your first proper day in London!

Uncle Ned

Next to the note was a small pile of coins and a key on a long piece of string. She tied it around her neck, drank the orange juice in one gulp, and snatched up the bread to eat as she walked. Tucking Special into her dungarees pocket, Fern headed out barefoot to explore her new neighbourhood.

Dandelion Road was a line of tiny houses with front doors painted in all the colours of the rainbow. Each house had a very short front garden and two front steps, but some of the houses had frothy curtains and some had plain, some had gardens filled with lots of flowers while others had only pebbles; one had a large statue of a dragon with water spouting out of its mouth. Fern liked the way that all of the houses looked exactly the same and yet totally different at the same time.

As she walked, chewing her bread and jam, she tried to imagine who might live in each house. Did they have pets? What jobs did they do? What did they do on the weekends when they didn't do what they did for their jobs? Were there – and this felt a little scary to be thinking about – any children living behind those brightly painted front doors?

She crossed the road and ran her hand along a row of railings until they found a gate. Behind it was the park she had seen from Blossom's taxi. The grass was patchy and dry, the flower beds were empty apart from some old bottles and a plastic bag, but none of that mattered to Fern because she could see trees: two tall ones huddled together in the corner. She let herself in and ran across the grass, her feet happy to be feeling something natural again after so many hours on a carpeted floor.

Reaching the trees, she flung her arms around the first one and squeezed it tight. "I didn't know if I would find anything like *you* in a city."

"It's not going to answer you back, is it? It's just a tree."

She turned around and saw a boy sitting cross-legged on a flat rectangle of concrete behind the trees. He was looking right at her.

She took a couple of steps towards him. There were two piles of small wooden pieces in front of him and, as she watched, he picked up one of the pieces and slotted it into a square frame.

"What are you doing?" she asked curiously.

"A jigsaw, of course." He held another piece up, swivelled it around a few times in front of his face, and then placed it in the frame.

"What's a jigsaw?" This time when he looked at her his expression was confused.

"Have you never done a jigsaw before?"

She shook her head. He looked her up and down as

if she was one of his pieces and he was trying to work out where to fit her.

"Are you Ned's niece?"

"How do you know?"

"I live next door. Ned said to my ajee that you were coming to live with him and you'd been brought up in the wilds. It must have been terrible. So where exactly are you from?"

"From?"

He nodded. "Everyone has to be from somewhere."

Fern wasn't sure she had an answer, not a simple one anyway. She had never really given any thought to where she came from. Her dad was from Scotland, her mum from New Zealand. But she hadn't been to either of those places since she was a baby.

Fern looked down now at the bits of her she could see. She was wearing a yellow dress bought in a market in Mexico when they were on a cactus-hunting trip, a hair clip bought on an Alpine plant trip in Switzerland, and the forget-me-not necklace her mum had given her at the airport before that awful goodbye.

"I suppose I'm from nowhere," she said at last, more to herself than to the boy.

"Nowhere isn't a place." He picked up a piece again and continued with the jigsaw.

Fern shrugged. "Are you from here?"

"My family has lived in our house for fifty years. Ajee says that we've been there so long that our roots grow deep below the floor of the house."

Fern wondered if you had to live somewhere for fifty years to be from somewhere. That meant she wouldn't really be from somewhere for a long, long time – maybe never.

An alarm went off from somewhere on the boy's wrist, and he smiled, gathering the bits of jigsaw into a box and standing up.

"Ajee makes me come out here every day even though she knows I hate it in the park, surrounded by all this horrible greenness. She says I need the fresh air. I think if people needed so much fresh air, we wouldn't have built houses in the first place."

He hitched the bag onto his shoulder. "I'll probably see you again, seeing as we're neighbours and all. I'm Woody, by the way." And then he ran across the park, lifting his feet high as if he was scared that the grass might bite him.

CHAPTER ELEVEN

Alone again, Fern turned to face the trees. If there was such a thing as feeling tree-sick, then that was what she had been feeling, ever since that horrible day in the Amazon when she had stopped climbing trees to try and convince her parents not to send her away.

"Would you mind terribly if I climbed you?" she asked, but the tree didn't answer back.

Looking up through its canopy, Fern wondered when adults like her parents stopped climbing. Did they just decide one day that trees were only to be looked at in books, or painted, or photographed? Did they wake one morning and find their feet had stopped itching altogether and wanted to stay where they were, firmly stuck to the ground? Did their toes simply stop dreaming?

If that was the case, she hoped she never had to grow up.

She spun around the two trees in a circle, her eyes searching out the branches and working out a climbing map. A tree that was good for climbing was strong but it also had an even spread of branches. Some trees just weren't built for climbing, however much you wanted to.

"I think I'll pick you," she said at last, pointing to the left-hand tree. "I don't want to offend you," she said apologetically, turning to the one on the right, just in case it did understand what she was saying. "But I can only choose one."

Pulling herself up on her tiptoes like a ballet dancer, she lifted her hands over her head – but even the lowest branches were far above her fingertips, tantalizingly out of reach. She lowered her feet again and took a step back and looked at the tree, her eyes narrowed in concentration. She saw now that the two trees grew so close to each other that some of their branches were entwined.

"You're like an old married couple holding hands! I wonder if your roots are twisted into each other underneath the ground too? Maybe that's my answer: to climb both of you."

She pulled Special up so the little plant was poking out of the top of her pocket and could enjoy the climb with her.

"Ready?" she said, and Special nodded eagerly. She stretched out her arms and put a hand on both of the trunks, feeling the scaly layers of grey and olive-coloured wood beneath her fingers. Pushing into the trees, she let her hands take her weight and jumped her feet up until she was wedged between them both, and then she began to organize herself upwards, feet pushing in firmly as her hands explored. As the lowest branch drew nearer, she reached and grabbed it with one hand, swinging the second one to follow it. Then, light as a feather, she plunged into the leafy heart of the tree without a backwards glance.

It was like entering a green cave. Her hands prodded, touched and tested branches as she pulled herself up, her feet winkled out friendly nodules, hidey-holes and toe rests from which she could push on up to the next branch. Her muscles were stretching like rubber bands, her breath coming in short, sharp gasps – she hadn't felt this happy for days.

Pausing in a fork between two branches, she stopped to rest, careful not to step on a nest that was perched there. She could see shards of pale blue shells – it must recently have been a nursery for baby birds.

Then she was off again, and as she climbed so did her shadow, which looked like it was dancing on the tree trunk in front of her, teasing and taunting her.

Up, up, up, it seemed to be saying. *Race you to the top, top, top!*

The higher they went, the quieter it got. The only noise here was her own breathing and the occasional peep from a surprised bird.

Finally, the last branch was above her and it looked thick enough to hold her. She placed a leg on each side as if she was sitting on a rocking horse, then she took Special out and propped the plant on her lap so it could get some fresh air and sunshine.

Far below her a cat sat on a roof lazily licking its paws, watched suspiciously by a pigeon on the next roof along. But the cat was enjoying the long-forgotten sunshine too much to be bothered with chasing.

She swung her eyes down to the other side of the park and beyond to a twirling church spire and then to a school playground, and at this point she almost toppled off the branch in surprise. There was an enormous green spiky thing taking over most of the skyline. Dad had told her there was a building in London called the Gherkin, but this was no building. Taller than the houses, it was fat and succulent and had spikes that looked like javelins. This was a plant.

"Do you think that was planted by that Guerrilla Gardener Blossom was talking about?" she said to

Special, feeling a strange tingling feeling in her throat. When she looked down, Special had ducked under her arm, and by the time she had managed to tease it out again, it was shaking with fear.

CHAPTER TWELVE

"Really. How big? Goodness me. Quite terrifying. I can see that, yes."

Uncle Ned was perched on the corner of the kitchen table talking on the phone. "Glad that you survived. Yes indeed, let me know if you find one. Doesn't it just!"

He put the phone down and waved at Fern who was lurking by the kitchen door. "That was my friend Briar Burdock with *quite* the story. He was out for tea at the Baker Street Tea Rooms where he goes every Tuesday; he finds it is the best place to write his murder mysteries. Anyhow, he was just tucking into a scone – they do make very good ones there, feather-light yet buttery, and the chef's own strawberry jam – when the building started to *tremble*!"

Uncle Ned's eyes widened as his enormous eyebrows headed up towards his hairline. "The cakes and sandwiches were catapulted from the stand onto

the ceiling and poor Burdock suffered a direct hit of egg mayonnaise to the eye."

"Poor Mr Burdock. I hope he's all right?"

"He is, Fern dear, he is. Things could have been much worse; apparently he narrowly missed a flying fork puncturing his nose. But I am happy to report he is unharmed."

"Why did the building tremble?" London really was *such* a strange place.

"It turns out that a few nights ago, someone – we can only guess that it must have been that insufferable Guerrilla Gardener chap – planted mint outside Sherlock Holmes's house, and in just a few short days it had grown so tall it was dwarfing the famous façade and the tea rooms next door. The management were rather pleased: it was apparently good for business and making the whole place smell divine – they had even started selling freshly picked mint tea with delicious baklava pastries which were a big hit. But –" he paused here for dramatic effect, clearly enjoying the storytelling – "unbeknown to them it had spread *considerable* roots beneath the hotel. Mint plants are terribly invasive, it seems. Gardeners have to plant them in pots in the ground to stop them taking over, and since this plant had grown roots as big as sewer tunnels, it caused an *earthquake*."

He pulled a handkerchief out of his pocket and dabbed it at his forehead. "Poor Burdock is beside himself; he has no idea where he will write on Tuesdays now. I just don't know what to make of it all, Fern." He went quiet, and hugged a mug of tea to himself like a comfort blanket.

Fern was used to enormous plants – she had spent most of her life being dwarfed by trees and bushes and flowers – but this definitely wasn't normal for London. She didn't know much about cities, but she knew that.

Sitting down, Fern pulled *The Grapevine* towards her, and flicked through it. On page seven there was a photo of another plant, this one a huge honeysuckle, draped over a building called the East London Mosque. It looked like it was strangling the golden dome and proud minarets of the beautiful building. She shivered, feeling the same funny feeling in her throat she'd had when she'd seen that huge spiky plant from the tree.

Uncle Ned interrupted her thoughts. "I am staying awake to go to the library this afternoon for research purposes, and I had thought to take you with me, but in rather exciting news, you have been invited to play with another child."

He pushed a plate of toast across the newly cleared table and she helped herself to a piece, buttering it crossly. She had already planned her day and it involved teaching Special some tricks with the marble; she had been busy in her room all morning making it a tiny tennis racquet.

"Who with?"

"The boy who lives next door – our neighbour, Woody. His granny tells me he could do with the company and it would be nice for you to have a companion to spend the summer holidays with, much more fun than your boring old uncle."

Fern's heart sank. "I don't want to," she said grumpily.

"I thought you would be pleased." Uncle Ned's face fell so much his glasses dropped off and landed with a clatter on the kitchen table. Fern hadn't meant to hurt his feelings – but she couldn't very well tell him she only wanted to play with her plant. Uncle Ned was different to his brother in lots of ways, but she didn't think he would believe her if she said she had a plant that understood her.

Still, she felt awful that he'd put in such an effort to make her feel at home. She took a deep breath. "I suppose, just this once."

Uncle Ned's face brightened instantly.

"Excellent! I am sure you will have fun! Woody seems like a nice young boy." He whipped the plates off the table and put them in the sink. "Now, I have six books on order, which means I have one space left on my ticket. May I get a book for you?"

Despite her reluctance to read her dad's old textbooks, Fern loved stories; dragon ones and mermaid ones, adventure stories and sad stories, tales about animals and about children from different countries all over the world. So, it surprised her when she said, "Please could I have a book on plants? A botany book."

Uncle Ned's eyebrows took flight in astonishment.

"When your father wrote to me and asked if you might stay here, he mentioned that you would not take your studies seriously. It sounds like London is already having a positive effect on you!"

"I suppose it is," Fern replied, quietly. She tucked her fingernails into her palms and dug them in, cross at herself for lying yet again. But she was so terribly curious about what Special was – and where it came from.

"I will see what I can do." He looked at the clock on the kitchen wall. "I must get there before two o'clock. Fatima Foxglove, a local romance writer, favours the same table as me, so I need to arrive before she commandeers the whole thing. Although she does bring chocolate biscuits, which we eat without the librarian knowing." He smiled mischievously, and Fern thought that maybe Uncle Ned might have a slight soft spot for his library friend.

An impatient *toot* from the street outside made them both jump.

"Ah, Blossom!" he said, gathering a few things in a plastic bag and slotting his wallet into the pocket of his jacket. Then he looked at her and coughed in embarrassment.

"Perhaps you might make yourself look a little … presentable. To make a good impression. Perhaps you could, ah, change out of that rather green-smeared T-shirt, and might I suggest wearing … some shoes?" Then he was gone, flitting excitedly down the garden path and into the waiting taxi.

"I might be in a new place but that doesn't mean I have to change who I am," Fern said furiously to Special, who watched as she shrugged on a fresh pair of dungarees. She left her shoes where they were, tucked under the empty bed frame.

"You're going to have to come with me. I'm not leaving you, there might be more earthquakes." But Fern was surprised to find that the plant couldn't squeeze into her dungarees pocket any more. No matter which way she turned it, it wouldn't fit. There was no denying that the little plant had grown in the last few days. She was going to have to repot it, and if she was going to take it with her, then she would have to find a different way to transport it.

She scanned the kitchen, looking for where might she find a flowerpot, but it was hard to see anything under the veil of white paper that lay over every surface. A large cupboard took up almost an entire wall – its missing front leg had been replaced with a pile of hardback books.

Fern opened the doors to a higgledy-piggledy mess. Uncle Ned seemed to be storing lots of old marmalade jars and ice-cream tubs, and there was also a flamingo feather, a box of candles, a mug full of old felt-tips without lids, and several bundles of paper tied with string. There were jam pots and honey pots but she couldn't see any plant pots.

Just as she was about to give up, she spotted something – not the kind of pot she was looking for, but a pot nonetheless. Tucked in the bottom corner of the cupboard was a small red teapot-for-one with a cracked spout. She turned excitedly to Special who was waiting on the table. "This might do just perfectly, what do you think?"

Fern was no expert on root growth, but as she eased Special out of the seedling pot, she was surprised to find that it didn't seem to have any roots at all. She fetched a few handfuls of soil from the garden, poured them into the teapot, then tucked Special into it and patted it down tenderly. Finally, she put the teapot in her plant-hunting bag and did up the buckles.

The bag immediately began to move, little bulges appearing all over it. She opened the buckles and peered inside.

"What's the matter? Don't you like it in there?" The plant shook its pod sadly. "Are you scared of the dark? Plants like light, don't they?" She went back to the wonky cupboard and found a torch and tied it to the inside of her bag with some of Uncle Ned's manuscript string. Then she filled one of the marmalade jars with water in case Special got thirsty. She stood back and looked proudly at her handiwork. Her dad had said the plant-hunting bag might come in useful in a city, but he couldn't have imagined how.

"There, now you have everything you need. You must promise me that you'll stay *very* quiet so nobody knows you're in there. I don't especially want to see Woody – but I'm quite sure he doesn't want to see you either."

CHAPTER THIRTEEN

A lady with badger-striped hair was waiting in the garden of number sixty-nine, fizzing with excitement. Fern felt a small shove in her back and found she was being propelled through the open door.

"My grandsonny is so excited! I am Woody's ajee, but everyone calls me Halo on account of me being practically perfect." Her mouth crinkled, showing off crooked white teeth, the tops of which were chipped like old porcelain mugs.

Fern remembered her manners and put her hand out to shake Halo's, but it was ignored and she was instead swamped in a hug that smelled of freshly baked bread and laundry powder.

"With all these crazy-mad things that have been happening in our city lately the poor boy hardly leaves the house any more." She let go and leaned towards Fern's face, whispering loudly so that Fern felt a light dusting of spittle on her cheek. "Don't mention that

earthquake, will you, or that terrifying cactus by his school swings, or we'll never get him through the gates again. Lord knows he needs the schooling, else all he will do is those jiggysaws he loves. I had to cancel our *Grapevine* subscription so he don't read all about it. Now you go on up, chicken, don't be shy!"

There was another sharp nudge in her back and Fern was propelled up the stairs, the plant-hunting bag bumping on her back with each step.

She had never been inside another child's bedroom and so she had no idea what to expect, though she might have imagined a messy space like her own corner of the family tent. But as she opened Woody's door, she was hit with a scent of freshly cut wood, and she stepped into a perfectly immaculate room. Boxes of jigsaws lined each of the walls like coloured bricks, and there were more stowed under the bed and several in neat piles on top of the wardrobe.

Woody was standing at the foot of the bed.

"Hello," he said matter-of-factly.

"Hello," she said.

"Why is your bag glowing?" Fern looked down and saw a dim light shining through the gaps in the stitched seams.

"Oh, that's nothing." Fern spun the bag around to her back, blushing.

"I thought we could do a jigsaw," Woody said awkwardly. "I picked one of my favourites."

By his feet was a box with a picture of an Egyptian pyramid in a desert. But Fern didn't really want to spend time in this strangely tidy room. She felt she was making it untidy just by being in it.

"It's not raining, so we could play in your garden instead?" she suggested. Maybe he had a proper garden unlike Uncle Ned's neglected patch.

"Gardens are dangerous places." Woody's eyes blinked rapidly. "You never know what might happen in one."

He kneeled down by the box and tipped it over. Hundreds of yellow pieces scattered across the carpet like petals.

"It takes ages and ages to do this one," he said, sounding pleased. With a silent sigh Fern gave in and sat beside him. Was this one of the complicated friendship rules that she'd never had to learn? Perhaps when you played at somebody's house, they always picked what you played.

"What do we do?" she said, trying to sound cheerful.

"Simple," he said. "You fit all the pieces together in the right place and make the photo on the box."

Wondering what the fun was in that, Fern picked

out two pieces, looked at them and then put them on the carpet in front of her.

"No!" Woody sounded a bit panicked. "Not like that. You always have to start with a plan. First, we sort all the pieces into piles. Straight edges over there, non-straight edges over here." His fingers raked through the pieces at lightning speed, until they were all collected into two neat piles.

"Then we sort those piles into different colours." He started dividing the two piles again.

"But aren't they all yellow?"

"Not all yellows are the same, you aren't looking closely enough."

Fern scrunched up her eyes. They still looked all the same to her. Woody picked one out and placed it on the ground in front of him.

"Now we begin!" he said excitedly.

Fern picked out a piece, but he grabbed her hand. "You won't be able to fit that one in yet, we're nowhere near ready." He dived back into the pile and grabbed a second piece and then, spinning it round and round in his hand, he fitted it into the first.

She tried with another one, but Woody batted it out of her hand before she could place it. In the end she gave up and just watched as he slotted in piece after piece, the tip of his tongue poking through his lips in concentration. Occasionally he would groan when he picked up a difficult one, then make a pleased noise when he managed to fit it in.

Jigsawing was definitely not a good spectator sport. Fern would have had much more fun at home playing with Special, but she hadn't even dared open her bag to peek at it in case it did something silly and gave the game away.

An hour later, Woody sat back, allowed himself a brief smile of victory, and then began to break the picture and throw the pieces back in the box.

"What is the fun in making something and breaking it again?" she wondered out loud. Woody's face looked thunderous.

"Ned said you were not very used to people but he never said you were rude."

"Well, you won't have to put up with me for long," Fern said huffily, stopping short of explaining to him that she had a running-away plan, because of course she didn't, not yet anyway. And even if she had, she wouldn't have told him about it.

Fern was more than ready to leave, but sitting down for so long had left her legs feeling a bit like marshmallows. As she stood up, she wobbled, knocking her plant-hunting bag so that the teapot rolled out and pitched onto its side.

Special wiggled in distress at finding itself the wrong way up.

Woody yelped, leaping backwards in horror. "What is that horrible thing?"

Fern picked up the teapot, dusted the bits of soil from it and clutched it tightly to her chest. Woody's eyes looked like they might actually pop out of his head and his breath was coming in short, sharp gasps.

"Get it away from me."

"Why are you being so silly? It's just a little plant."

"Don't you understand?"

"Understand what?"

"I'm botanophobic!" he cried.

CHAPTER FOURTEEN

"Botanawhatty?"

What was Woody talking about? He was pressed up against the bedroom wall, covering his mouth with his hand.

"Botanophobic. I have a phobia of plants. I am scared of them, really scared." Although his voice was muffled, she could still hear it trembling.

"You shouldn't be scared of plants, they won't hurt you! They suck in all the carbon dioxide we make and give out oxygen so that we can breathe. How can you be scared of something clever like that?" She patted Special, hoping that it hadn't taken offence. "That's just not sensible."

"There is nothing sensible about phobias," Woody said. "To me plants smell scary and they feel disgusting and you never know if they might be poisonous…" He turned to face them but didn't move any closer. "My anxiety finds all sorts of ways to show itself, mostly

88

in ways that people don't even try to understand."

Special reached a tendril in Woody's direction as if telling him that it wasn't any of those things and he didn't need to be scared. He pushed back against the wall as though the plant was trying to attack him! Fern patted Special on the pod to remind it to behave.

"What *is* it?" he whispered.

"It's my pet plant," she said proudly. "It's called Special."

"You gave a plant a name?"

"Of course," she said. "All plants have names, but they are usually in Latin, and I'm not very good at Latin, so I chose a name that suited it instead."

"Is it a he or a she?" Woody asked, leaning closer despite himself, peering at the pod which was now the size of a golf ball.

"Plants are much more diverse and exciting than that," Fern said. "Sometimes they are a he, sometimes they are a she, sometimes they are a he *and* a she. I don't know what gender Special is but I like it whatever it is."

Woody was looking at its little spear now, which had grown longer and slightly fearsome-looking.

"That looks really sharp."

"Don't touch it, then."

"The last thing I would do is touch a plant!" He

visibly shuddered at the thought. "Did your parents give it to you?"

Fern paused. She didn't know very much about other children but she felt sure that telling someone you were a thief as soon as you met them probably wasn't a good idea. So, for once, she thought carefully before she spoke.

"I found it on one of our trips." It wasn't exactly a lie, more a smudging of the truth.

Woody didn't seem to notice that her cheeks were glowing at the edges. But he had noticed that the plant label had fallen by his feet and after a quick nudge with his trainer, he picked it up. "*The Magnolia Hotel*," he read. "Why does it say that?"

"I don't think that's important." Fern didn't want any more questions about where Special came from.

"There is something … familiar about that name." His tongue pushed out his cheek thoughtfully. At that moment, Special reached out a tendril and pulled the label from his hands and Woody let out another yelp.

"Can you take that disgusting thing *away* from me, please?" Fern could see that his back was shaking so much that his shirt was rippling. Why was he being so ridiculous? Enough was enough.

She ran down the stairs and out the front door, slamming it behind her. If Special wasn't welcome then she was never coming here again.

"Well, jigsaws *are* boring, aren't they?" Fern said when they were back in her bedroom. "If that's what it's like having a friend, well, then, Mum was wrong. I don't need one. He's just a stupid, ignoran— Ow!"

Special's spike brushed roughly against her arm as if telling her off. Tears stung Fern's eyes as a spot of blood appeared. In the blink of an eye, its pod leaped towards the blood spot, the little mouth snapping hungrily.

"Stop it, you're being silly now," she giggled, but she wasn't entirely sure the plant was joking. When she finally managed to prise it away from her, it hung its pod as if now telling *itself* off for something.

Special unfurled one of the coils below its pod into a leaf, and brushed it across her face by way of an apology.

"I forgive you. We all do silly things sometimes. Now, what shall we do until Uncle Ned gets back?"

She looked around the room for inspiration, her eyes settling on the large cardboard box that he still hadn't gotten round to moving. Could there be anything interesting in there?

Inside she found a pile of colourful cardboard sleeves and, lurking beneath them, an ancient-looking machine. Easing it out, she saw that it had a moveable arm and a round part that spun when she pushed it.

Sliding a black shiny disc from one of the sleeves, she decided that it must be something to do with the machine, but it took several goes to work out how.

"Ha, Woody! You're not the only one who can solve puzzles." She clicked a button and the disc started turning and music filled the room.

"Ah ha! You've found my old record player! Turn it off, though, will you? I can't hear myself think down here!" Uncle Ned called from downstairs. Fern hadn't heard him come in the front door.

But Fern didn't want to turn it off yet. The music was having a strange effect on Special. It flung its tendrils to the side and waved them in time to the beat, then it jiggled its stem and shook its leaves to one side and then the other. But when she started to laugh it stopped.

"Sorry, I didn't mean to embarrass you. Please, keep going!"

As she watched, she felt an itch in her own toes. She hadn't wanted to dance since she left the Amazon, but her feet seemed to be insisting, and soon she was moving and swaying around the room. As she passed Special she snatched it up and lifted the plant above her head, and they spun around and around until they were both dizzy.

Sinking down on to her duvet, she balanced the teapot on her knees.

"You remind me so much of my old life, my life before London. You are my secret wild."

She dragged out her sketchbook from its hiding place under the mattress.

"The sooner you meet my parents, the better. When Dad realizes that plants like you exist, he'll want to go on a trip to hunt out more plants just like you. I need to finish my running-away plan so we can get back to them. You'll have to stop growing, though, or you'll never fit on the plane!"

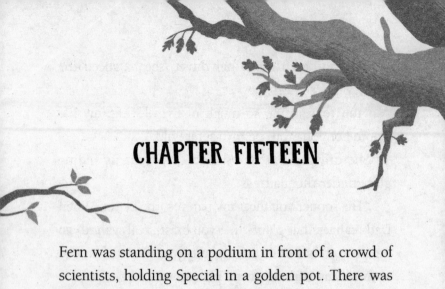

CHAPTER FIFTEEN

Fern was standing on a podium in front of a crowd of scientists, holding Special in a golden pot. There was a medal around her neck and she could see her parents in the front row, clapping. She had never seen that expression on her father's face before, one of pride and wonder when he looked at his daughter.

Then, with a sharp tug, the medal was being pulled from her neck, and she saw the botanist from the plane in front of her. She felt Special being pulled from her hands, and it flailed as if it was hurting. She let go but it was too late and, with a sound like fraying rope, Special snapped in half.

Fern's eyes flung open in horror and relief flooded her body as she realized she was lying on top of her feathery duvet on the floor, sketchbook open beside her. She must have fallen asleep. She turned her head to say good morning to Special and saw that its stem was arched over, pod resting on the floorboards.

"How sweet. Is that how you sleep?" she asked, but the plant didn't pop up at the sound of her voice. Moving towards it, she saw that the leaf that had appeared yesterday now drooped at its side, and the two tendrils were wrapped around its stem as if it was hugging itself.

"Do you feel sick, Special?"

She jumped up and filled a toothbrush mug with water and trickled it ever so gently over Special, but that only seemed to make it droop even more.

Fern felt the first nudge of panic. What had her father said about looking after their specimens? She shut her eyes and squeezed her forehead muscles together until she could hear his sharp voice saying, *"moisture, temperature, food"*.

She opened her eyes and buried her finger in the soil of the pot. "It feels just right; not too damp, not too dry. It's not hot in here and it isn't cold, so I think the temperature is right too. So, you're hungry, you must be. Why didn't I think about that?"

More of her dad's words flooded into her brain. "Plants can't live on water alone, Fern. Once you take a plant from the ground and put it in a pot you take away its ability to feed itself."

Guilt began to trickle over her. She was a terrible plant owner. She hadn't thought of this when she'd stolen a sweet baby plant on a plane, she had thought only of herself, of wanting something to cheer her up and call her own. She hadn't thought about whether she would be able to look after it properly.

"I'll make it better, I promise you." She massaged its pod with her finger, feeling just the smallest bit of pressure in return, as if the plant was leaning into her finger for comfort. "If I can find out what kind of plant you are, then I'll know what to feed you."

She rushed down the stairs to the hall. By the pointy feet of the suit of armour was Uncle Ned's pile of library books, and sandwiched between a book on medieval castles and one about equine armour, she found a thick-spined book with the title: *Bert Beetle's Botany for Beginners*.

The picture on the front cover was of a jolly looking man with a bushy beard and a bald head and clumps of hair coming out of his ears like fireworks.

She ran her hand down the list of chapters, then skimmed through the pages until she reached chapter twenty-one: 'Feeding Your Plant'.

She took a deep breath and began to read.

*Always ensure that the type of food you are giving is the right one, matched carefully to the plant you are feeding. *A feed should be well-*

*balanced. *Nitrogen, phosphorus, potassium, magnesium, sulphur and calcium, given in the right amounts, will help a plant to grow properly, flower well and build resistance to disease. *Your plants will always be grateful to you.*

She shut the book smartly, waiting for the familiar feeling of restlessness that always hit her when she opened her dad's books. But Bert Beetle stared back at her from the cover in a kind way, as if he was willing her to keep going, so she opened the book again and flicked through every page. There were lots of colourful pictures that made reading it much easier than Dad's boring old books, but there was not a single plant that looked anything like Special. How could she find the right food for her plant if she had no idea what it actually was?

Back upstairs, Special was looking even limper, and had started to change colour to a parched green, as if it was drying out. She tried to feed it a fly, hoping that counted as food, but Special didn't even try and take it from her finger. She flashed the torch a few times and trickled some water on it again. Neither seemed to help. Slumping against the wall, it felt like she had exhausted all her ideas.

Then, like the sun coming out from behind the

clouds, her mind cleared and she knew what she needed to do.

"I don't think you're going to be in any book, Special. You are too unique for that. The only person who can tell me what you need is the botanist I took you from." The last time Fern had seen her was driving away in a van, and London was a huge place – how would she track down one person? She didn't even know her name.

Then she remembered the tag tucked into the teapot – of course! *The Magnolia Hotel*. But still, she had no idea how to get there alone.

She slipped it into her dungarees pocket, wrapped Special in a flannel to keep it warm and moist, and popped it into her plant-hunting bag. Then she stuck her desert hat on her head.

It was time to say sorry.

CHAPTER SIXTEEN

There was something stuck in Halo's hair, and it took Fern a few moments to realize that it was a piece of cucumber.

"Fern, sweetheart!" she said, a smile breaking across her face like a gentle wave. "Did you and my grandsonny have fun yesterday? You must have, if you're back so soon!"

Luckily, before Fern had to tell a lie, there was a crashing noise from the back of the house.

"I'd better not be leaving them too long or they'll be burning the house down. Come in."

"Leave who?" But Halo was already hurrying along the corridor. Following her, Fern noticed that Woody's granny had a smear of something that looked like carrot on the back of her dress.

"I sent the boy out," Halo called back. "I told him I needed milk, but truth is he finds feeding time difficult. He's funny 'bout mess, you see, has been his whole life, and it's got worse since the babies were born."

"Babies?" That must be the noise she had heard through the thin walls of her bedroom.

"When he gets back, it's all spick and span and he can cope again. My papa was the same, I guess he inherited the gene."

The piece of cucumber dislodged from her hair and fell to the ground. "Who put that in there?" she laughed, opening the door into a kitchen. "It's like feeding a pack of wild animals in here, chicken."

Sitting in a row of high chairs at a kitchen table were three miniature Woodys, each wearing a selection of food on their faces. The floor, table and wall were also decorated with food. Fern swallowed a giggle. One of the babies made a noise like a cross buffalo and she just managed to dodge a piece of broccoli that came hurtling through the air towards her.

"Jackson, Joe and Juniper," said Halo, pointing at each one in turn. "Woody's triplet brothers. Jackson, you put that down. Hang on, you're not Jackson." She took a pea from his cheek. "It was hiding his birthmark, it's the only way I can tell them apart sometimes. That would be Joe."

"They are very sweet," said Fern because she thought it was probably the right thing to say, though truthfully they looked anything but sweet. They looked like three resting volcanos ready to blow at any minute.

Halo's laugh tinkled like wind chimes. "Perhaps if you come round one day five minutes after their bath, just before they go to bed, then, maybe, *just maybe*, you can call them sweet." She looked at them fondly, however, and was rewarded by one of them – was it Joe or Jackson? – tipping a full yoghurt pot onto the floor.

"Would you like to wait for Woody?"

A low-flying piece of satsuma whizzed past Fern's left ear.

"Erm, perhaps I'll…" Fern started to back out of the room to a chorus of banging spoons, but at that moment Woody came through the front door. Taking one look at the mess in the kitchen, he turned and ran up the stairs.

"Go after him," said Halo softly.

"What do you want?" Woody called as Fern followed him. He sat stiffly on his bed, a carton of milk in his hands, looking in no mood for idle chat. She came straight to the point.

"It's my plant. The one you met yesterday. I'm worried it's going to die."

She plonked down next to him on the bed.

"Why do you want *my* help?" Woody said. "I don't know anything about plants. I couldn't help you even if I wanted to."

"Yesterday you thought you recognised the name, *The Magnolia Hotel*? I wondered if you knew where it was."

Woody looked at her as if trying to work out whether she was worth helping or not, then finally he nodded. "I remembered where I'd seen the name last night." He fiddled with the button on his shirt. "My dad used to work in a jigsaw factory, the oldest one in Britain," he said proudly. "I sometimes went with him to work and he would let me sit under his desk while he cut out the jigsaws and I'd collect the sawdust into piles. I like organizing things, you see."

"What's that got to do with the hotel?" Fern didn't want to be rude, but she didn't feel like she had much time to spend listening to stories. There was a sick plant in her bag and it needed help.

"I'm getting to that. Next door to the factory there was a building I always noticed because it looked old and abandoned, and some of the other factory workers used to say it was haunted. They said it was a hotel, built by a rich Victorian who traded silk. My history teacher at school said the Victorians didn't just take treasures that belonged to the rest of the world, they also brought back plants for their gardens and glasshouses. I guess the hotel was named after a tree that he had brought back on one of his ships."

"The Magnolia Hotel?" Fern whispered and Woody nodded.

She felt her heart thud with a mixture of fear and excitement. She didn't know her way across London, even if she had a map (which she didn't), so there was no way she would find it alone.

"Could you take me there?"

Woody's fingers flew to his neck and he clasped it nervously. "I'm not sure. I'm needed at home. The triplets – I made a promise to my mum and dad that I'd help Ajee with them, and I can't break that and Mum's on a double shift at the hospital today. She's a doctor," he explained proudly. "Now that my dad isn't around..." He broke off and looked out of the window.

"Please, Woody? I don't know London at all, it looks like one giant maze to me."

Woody slipped the shirt button through the button hole and back again.

"I haven't got anyone else," she said. "I wouldn't ask you if it wasn't really, really important."

They sat in silence as Woody fiddled with his button.

"I suppose I can leave Ajee and the boys, just for a few hours."

The relief Fern felt was like a waterfall.

"Can we go now?"

He nodded and she stood up and held out her hand, which was something she had seen her dad do when he made an agreement. Woody looked at her hand as if it had warts all over it.

"It might be planty," he explained, wrinkling his nose.

CHAPTER SEVENTEEN

They walked side by side along Dandelion Road, though not close as friends would – there was daylight between them. It may have stopped raining, but tiny rivers of rainwater still ran down the middle of the road, and water had pooled at the sides.

"You've forgotten something!" said Woody suddenly. "Your shoes. You've forgotten your shoes."

"I haven't forgotten them. I just don't like wearing them," she said. "When I wear shoes, I feel like I have my clothes on back to front."

"But the roads are soaking. And you'll step on something. A nail or a piece of glass or ... something"

"I won't. Besides, my feet don't care about getting wet. In fact, they like it." She hopped into a puddle just to prove it to him. Woody looked horrified, but Fern skipped ahead happily, jumping from puddle to puddle until the bottom of her dungarees had to be rolled up.

"Which way are we going?" she asked after they had walked a few streets.

"We're going underground," he said, smiling for the first time since they had left his house.

Below ground it was muggy. As a train emerged from the dark of the tunnel mouth and clattered to a stop by the platform, Fern shivered. Being underground or in dark spaces had never suited her – she was always much happier in trees like the birds.

"We'll get on this one," Woody said, pulling her through the opening doors of a carriage.

Once they were inside, he took a small towel from inside his backpack, laid it on the seat and sat on it.

The train jumped forward and soon they were rumbling slowly through pitch-black tunnels. Fern wondered how deep underground they were. Deeper than worms? Deeper than mice? Deeper than badgers and foxes? There were wires running along the tunnel too, wires that ... moved? Wires didn't move, did they? She sat bolt upright.

Something was running along the tunnel wall and that something was *much* bigger than a wire, more like a fat pipe, and it was covered in *hairs*. Fern might not be a keen student of botany but she had been around plants long enough to know a root when she saw one.

She had never seen one *this* big. She turned and looked through the window on the other side of the carriage. There was another one.

And this one was definitely moving!

She felt her throat tighten as if the root was squeezing it. No wonder the roots were causing earthquakes if they were this enormous.

A passenger opposite them was hidden behind a copy of *The Grapevine*. The headline read:

PICCADILLY LINE CLOSED AFTER TUNNEL FALLS IN DUE TO ROOT INFESTATION AT LEICESTER SQUARE

Fern quickly pointed at a picture of jumbled lines on the carriage wall to distract Woody — and herself — from the headline. "That looks like someone gave your triplets a packet of felt-tip pens."

"*That* is the Underground map," said Woody. "Ned hasn't taught you anything about London, has he?"

"It's a mess." She turned her head to the side and tried to trace one of the lines from beginning to end.

"It's a masterpiece of organization actually — it turns chaos into perfect sense," he said with satisfaction. "Believe me, I don't like mess. We'll change there." He pointed at a dot that said *Elephant and Castle*.

"Will we see an elephant and a castle?" Fern asked

excitedly. Her dad had shown her pictures of the castles in Scotland – huge, grey, fearsome-looking buildings.

"Of course not," Woody said. "After that we'll hop on the Northern line." He pointed out a thick black line that ran straight up the map. "Then we get off and we can walk into the City."

"I thought we were in the city already."

"Not the city. *The* City. London is a city, but *the* City is where the buildings are as big as mountains and the bankers are as rich as kings and queens." Fern's eyes widened. "That's what my dad used to say on our journey in."

"There must be elephants and castles in the City, then, if everyone is so rich?" She tried to make a joke to cheer him up from whatever was making his eyes look sad. But he turned away to watch a busker playing a guitar further down the carriage.

Fern took the chance to quickly unbuckle her bag. She ran her finger along the pod that was peeking out from the top of the flannel and stroked it tenderly, hoping Special could tell how much she loved it.

There was a grinding screech as the train pulled up to a platform.

"*Elephant and Castle*," announced a tannoy. "*Please mind the gap.*" Fern followed Woody as, hand over his mouth, he led her through white-walled tunnels, up layers of stairs and then onto another train.

Then finally they were back above ground and Fern breathed in the sweet fresh air gratefully, trying to rid her nose of the smell of iron and sweat and strangers. Woody had said the buildings in the City were tall, but these were taller than she could have imagined, taller even than the gigantic redwood pines in California. How could these buildings stand up? How did they not topple down in a crumble of bricks and dust and window glass?

The people who passed them didn't look like kings and queens. They travelled somewhere between a walk and a run and were so busy that nobody even noticed the barefoot girl and the boy with his hand over his mouth.

"This way," Woody said, and then, "Over there," then, "Cross here," and Fern trailed after him as obediently as a puppy as they wound their way through the City.

"What is that enormous glass tower?" Fern said.

"That's the Shard," Woody said, not looking up. "As perfectly designed as the Underground map. Eight shards of white glass lean in to make the most elegant spire in the world."

"What's growing up it?" As quickly as the words were out of her mouth, Fern realized her mistake. Woody looked at the building and she saw him gulp.

Snaking up the sparkling glass was a gnarled plant with elephant ear leaves. It looked like a giant version of a philodendron she had seen in Thailand. A breeze whipped up from the Thames and spun around their shoulders as if it was warning them about something.

"Who would do that to the Shard?" Woody looked devastated and scared.

Fern felt the funny feeling in her throat again, as if something was tightening around it. She put her hand to her neck, but that didn't make it go away. She followed Woody in silence for another five minutes until he stopped at the edge of a pavement.

"The jigsaw factory," he said, his voice creaking slightly. Fern saw an old, low building which looked out of place nestled between the huge offices. It needed a fresh lick of paint but it had a friendly red door and a large sign with a picture of a tree and the words: *Willow Wood Jigsaws*. Woody was staring at it as if his memories were boxing with him.

"Did your dad die?" Fern asked before she could stop herself.

"Die?"

"You said that you promised him you would help your ajee once he couldn't." She examined his face anxiously, wondering if she had done the wrong thing by asking. Why wasn't there a friendship book that told you the right things to say and when to say them? It was all so confusing.

To her surprise and relief, Woody's face relaxed and he laughed.

"No, he's not dead! He's just not around as much as he used to be. My parents didn't know about the babies. I mean, they knew Mum was *pregnant*, that there was going to be a baby. I was so excited, I had wanted a brother or sister for ages. Everyone else seemed to have one and it was like a club that I couldn't join."

He frowned. "They found out, in the scan, that it was three babies. I can still remember the look on Dad's face, he was so scared and so pleased at the same time. But after that life had to change in every way. Dad loved his job at the jigsaw factory, he always said he was one of the only people he knew who came home from work as happy as he left in the morning. Problem is that making jigsaws the old-fashioned way doesn't pay much, so he had to find another job. Mum went back to work at the hospital as quickly as she could and Ajee offered to look after us. Then Dad found a new job as an engineer."

"That's good, isn't it?" Fern felt pleased that the story was a happy one after all.

"It's on an oil rig. In the sea. Off Scotland." His face looked as gloomy as a winter sea.

"Oh."

"He goes for a month at a time. He takes the train and then he has to fly on a big helicopter. He says it's really scary when the sea is rough and they have to land on the rig and the helicopter is being blown back and forth like a ping-pong ball."

Fern thought it sounded exciting – she had always wanted to go in a helicopter – but from the expression on Woody's face she could tell he didn't share her feelings, and that he worried about his dad.

"When he comes home we are so pleased to see him we have a party every time. Ajee bakes for four whole days and the house smells of cinnamon and sugar and excitement. Then when he gets here, when he walks through the door, everything is brilliant again." He smiled briefly but it slipped away just as quickly. "Then he sleeps for two days. I get cross with him. I miss him so much and I get cross that he just sleeps when he comes home and doesn't have time for me."

He stopped abruptly and looked at Fern. "Sorry, I forgot where I was for a minute. I don't talk to people about it much."

Fern wanted to say that it was fine, that she liked him talking to her, but he was already moving on. She looked thoughtfully at the back of his head. It was as if she had put on a pair of glasses that let her see him more clearly. Maybe they weren't so different after all. He knew what it was like to miss someone so much that you felt you had a hole on the inside. Could you be as different from someone as she and Woody were, and yet so similar at the same time?

"Come on, let me show you where this hotel is."

CHAPTER EIGHTEEN

At some point the Magnolia Hotel must have been beautiful. It stood four storeys tall and eight windows wide, and was built of buttery bricks that seemed to glow in the sunshine. You could tell that important people must have passed through the grand entrance once upon a time, but now the hotel's smudged brass sign was covered in so many cobwebs that it looked like it was wearing a crocheted shawl.

The tree from which it took its name stood outside the front door, branches adorned with teacup flowers, each of which a clever seamstress could have turned into a dress for a fairy. It was the type of building that made you dream about its past, but it was not the type of building that made you want to go inside. It looked like it was slowly rotting like an apple on a compost heap.

Fern's heart had a last-minute wobble. Did the botanist really have anything to do with this place?

Surely botanists should be in forests, or jungles, or at botanic gardens, not in the middle of a busy city. Would she find any clues about Special here?

"So what do you want to do now?"

Fern thought for a moment.

"I met a lady on a plane and I need to find something out from her about Special. I thought that she might be here." She watched his face for a reaction.

He began to walk towards a bench. "I don't want anything to do with a plant person. I'll wait for you outside. Good luck."

"I can't just walk in."

"Why not?"

Her throat felt dry. A seed of friendship had been sown on the train, and suddenly that mattered very much to her. What would Woody do if he knew she had been lying to him?

"I... Well... I probably should have told you before..."

"Told me what?"

"It's just ... I might have ... in fact, I did ... most definitely... I... I stole Special." She forced the last incriminating words out and they hung between them.

"You did *what*?" He looked amazed.

"Well, not *exactly* stole. More that I didn't put it back. It's not quite the same as stealing, is it?" She looked at him anxiously, hoping he might be able to make her feel better.

"Surely you know taking something that isn't yours is wrong even if you are a bit … you know … a bit wild."

"I know that, of course I do! It's just, I was … I was lonely," she admitted. "And I'm not *wild*, I just grew up differently to you."

Woody walked to the bench and sat on it with a disappointed *thud*, tucking his long legs under him. "Why didn't you tell me any of this?" He looked a little like he had been stung by a bee.

She shrugged. "I thought you might judge me."

He sighed, letting out a long breath. Then he opened his backpack and took out a package wrapped in newspaper that Halo had handed him when he told her they were going out.

"Ajee thinks if people go half an hour without eating they might fade away." He began to unwrap it. "Everything makes more sense after Ajee's butter cake."

He took a large slab of cake from inside the newspaper, broke it in two and handed a piece to her. Fern took a bite; it was sweet and buttery and delicious. But neither of them could ignore the photograph of a food shop on the newspaper page, so engulfed in leaves that nobody could walk through the door.

BAGELS BANISHED!

The appearance of goutweed inside the famous Beigel Bake Shop on Brick Lane has caused a power cut which has left the restaurant unable to serve their salt beef bagels for the first time since 1855. The Mayor of London, Dharma Dahlia, has called today for the formation of a specialist police squad on the ground to investigate the Guerrilla Gardener, and put a stop to the green menace which is spreading across the city and disrupting all Londoners' way of life. From today all lorries entering the city will be checked for giant plants.

Woody crumpled the newspaper angrily and threw it in the bin as if that would solve the problem. They finished their cake quietly, watching customers queuing by a coffee van that stood next to a flower stall, stacked with buckets of bright flowers.

"I'm worried if I go in there and tell her I have her plant that she will want it back," Fern managed to say at last. "But I have to find out more about Special because it's ill, Woody. Really ill. If I can just get inside the hotel without the botanist seeing me, then maybe… Well, maybe I can find something that will help."

At that moment Special found a smidgen of energy and poked a tendril out of the bag, like a sad octopus tentacle.

Woody jumped. "You didn't tell me you'd brought it with you." The tendril rested limply across Fern's leg.

"I couldn't leave it behind when it was so unwell. Special is all I've got."

"It *does* look ill," Woody said at last. He finished his cake and brushed the crumbs from his lap. "Well, as we're here, I suppose you should do something."

"Thank you, Woody." Fern felt a tingle, as if a little seedling of friendship had broken through the ground. She had told him her worst, most shameful secret and he hadn't run away.

"So, what's your plan?"

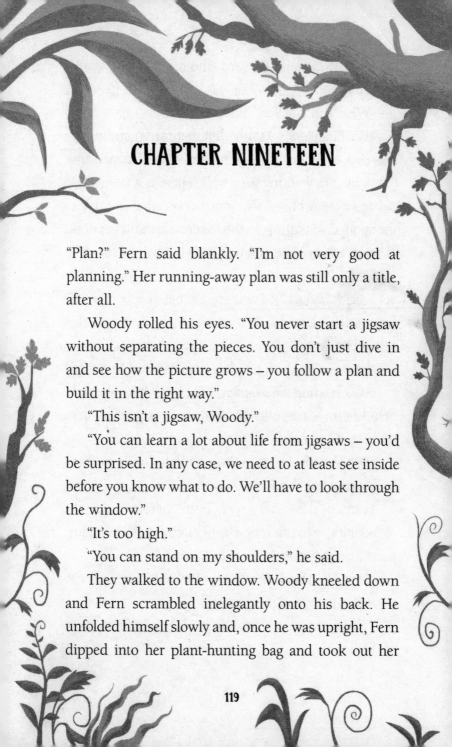

CHAPTER NINETEEN

"Plan?" Fern said blankly. "I'm not very good at planning." Her running-away plan was still only a title, after all.

Woody rolled his eyes. "You never start a jigsaw without separating the pieces. You don't just dive in and see how the picture grows – you follow a plan and build it in the right way."

"This isn't a jigsaw, Woody."

"You can learn a lot about life from jigsaws – you'd be surprised. In any case, we need to at least see inside before you know what to do. We'll have to look through the window."

"It's too high."

"You can stand on my shoulders," he said.

They walked to the window. Woody kneeled down and Fern scrambled inelegantly onto his back. He unfolded himself slowly and, once he was upright, Fern dipped into her plant-hunting bag and took out her binoculars. Leaning forward, she rested them against the window.

"What can you see?" he asked.

"The hotel lobby, I think. But there aren't any guests. It is sort of ... creepy looking and dark, I don't think the lights are working very well. There is a desk, a big old desk. Hang on—" She drew her breath in sharply as she spotted something in the shadows behind the desk. "There's a man." She grabbed Woody's hair in shock.

"Ow!"

"Sorry. It's just ... I've seen him before, the man. He was on the plane too. He works for the botanist. He's called Ginkgo."

"So we've got the right place then. What is he doing?"

"He's reading a newspaper. There's a staircase right behind him, a magnificent staircase. It must lead up to the rest of the hotel."

"Do you think we could get to the stairs without him seeing us?" he asked.

Fern pushed her eyes even harder into the binoculars, creating little steam circles on the window pane from her breath.

"No." She shook her head. "The only way to get to the stairs is to go right past him."

"There must be a way. Keep looking. Find a piece of the jigsaw."

Fern tried to ignore the noise of beeping horns and rushing people, and concentrate on what she could see in front of her. She watched as Ginkgo folded the paper away, rubbed his eyes and then opened the wrapped sandwich that sat next to him on the desk. He ate greedily, then took a handkerchief out of his pocket and blew his nose into it several times.

Rubbing his eyes again, he slid open a drawer in the desk and took out a small bottle. He squirted liquid into his eyes, one at a time, blinked several times, then put the bottle away and turned back to his newspaper.

"I've got it!" Fern said suddenly, making Woody wobble below her. She slid off his shoulders, knocking into his ear in her hurry.

"Ouch!" he said. "Got what?"

"I've got a plan. At least I think I have. Or I *hope* I have." She had never had a proper plan before so she wasn't really sure what they felt like.

"Come on, this way."

Fern pulled Woody to the flower stall, fumbling in her plant-hunting bag for her purse. She chose a bushy plant pot with purple flowers from the shelf and handed it to the stall holder who wrapped it in paper. She fished out four shiny pound coins, which he slotted into the pocket of his leather apron.

"You didn't tell me the plan involved more plants," said Woody nervously when they were out of earshot.

"The plant *is* the plan. Let's call it the outsides of the jigsaw and now we have to fill in the pieces." She grinned, heading back towards the hotel entrance again.

"Now, I just need to wait until I find another piece," she said.

Fern's eyes lit up as a red van approached them, lumbering onto the pavement.

"Got it!" A woman in blue shorts climbed out and by the time she had pulled a post bag from the back, Fern was beetling over to her.

"Excuse me, ma'am," she said in her most polite voice, holding the purple-flowered plant out in front of her. "I wonder if you could help me? I have to deliver this plant to the Magnolia Hotel, but I'm late. Really late, actually. I'm expected home for lunch, and I wondered if you would be *so* kind, whether you could deliver it with the mail please?"

The postwoman looked at her, then at the plant, and then at her again. "Anything for such a polite girl. Hand it over, then. I'm always delivering unusual things in there."

She took the plant and disappeared inside. Fern pulled Woody back towards the window.

"What are you planning?"

She put her finger to her lips to quiet him, and then clambered back onto his shoulders. As she watched, the postwoman took a handful of letters and gave them to Ginkgo, then placed the plant on the desk. Fern saw her lips move as he said something to him and Ginkgo nodded.

"The first bit has worked," she whispered.

As the postwoman walked back across the lobby, Ginkgo's face reddened. He launched into a thundering volley of sneezes that Fern could hear even through the thick walls.

"What's going on?" Woody said from below.

"It's working!" she said in disbelief. "My plan is working!"

Ginkgo's eyes were watering and liquid was spluttering from his nose as he launched into another round of sneezes that shook the chair he was sat on.

"I'm going in!" shouted Fern, sliding from Woody's back and running to the door. To her enormous surprise, he followed her.

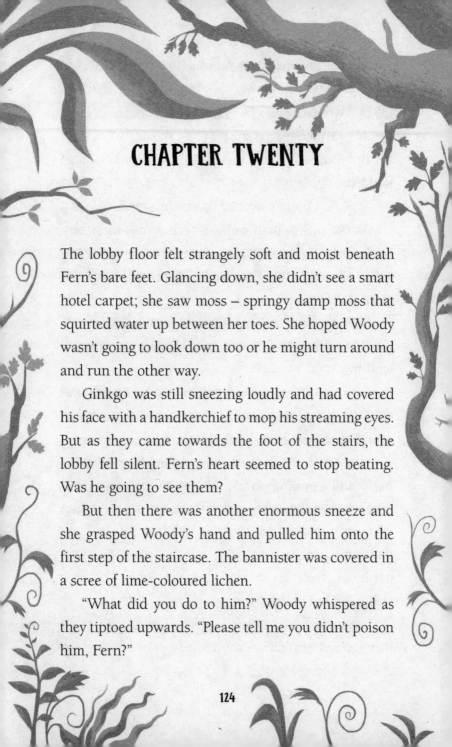

CHAPTER TWENTY

The lobby floor felt strangely soft and moist beneath Fern's bare feet. Glancing down, she didn't see a smart hotel carpet; she saw moss – springy damp moss that squirted water up between her toes. She hoped Woody wasn't going to look down too or he might turn around and run the other way.

Ginkgo was still sneezing loudly and had covered his face with a handkerchief to mop his streaming eyes. But as they came towards the foot of the stairs, the lobby fell silent. Fern's heart seemed to stop beating. Was he going to see them?

But then there was another enormous sneeze and she grasped Woody's hand and pulled him onto the first step of the staircase. The bannister was covered in a scree of lime-coloured lichen.

"What did you do to him?" Woody whispered as they tiptoed upwards. "Please tell me you didn't poison him, Fern?"

"Pollen," she said simply. "That plant is a member of the *Asteraceae* family, known for their high pollen count."

He looked confused.

"Hay fever," she explained. "My mum suffers from it, which is why it's about the only Latin name I can remember. Ginkgo seemed to be having the same symptoms. Did you see he was squirting something into his eyes? My mum does that too. I took a chance!"

"I thought hay fever was from grass?" said Woody nervously as if he had found a whole new thing to worry about.

"Not all hay fever is caused by wind pollination, some can come direct from flowers." She was surprised by how expert she sounded.

As the staircase curved around, they saw a grand doorway ahead of them. Fern and Woody looked at one another.

"Shall we?" she said.

"Should we?" he said, more anxiously.

Fern nodded, and, not having the smallest idea what they might find beyond, they stepped through the doors, standing so close together that there was hardly an inch of daylight between them. The door clanged shut behind them.

Fern's nose got its bearings first. The circular room they entered smelled like the damp floor of an evergreen forest or like a jungle after a rainstorm. It wasn't an unpleasant smell exactly, but it was an unusual one for the inside of a building.

As her eyes adjusted from the bright sunlight outside, she saw what must once have been a very grand ballroom, with an ornate but slightly saggy ceiling. There might have been pretty paint or patterns on the walls at one time, but now they were decorated with tea-stain patches, and delicate strands of ivy poked through gaps in the plaster and crept across the walls like living wallpaper.

There was the sound of dripping water from the corner. "A fountain!" Fern said in surprise. Water was being spat out of a stone mermaid and it was pooling into a curved bowl, around which moisture-loving plants had sprouted; flat-leaved hart's tongue grew next to spidery-looking maidenhair spleenwort and bright ivy-leaved toadflax. "Why don't we get you a drink, Special? You've been in there such a long time."

On catching sight of Fern, a frog slunk beneath the surface, staring grumpily up at her through the water. As she bent to scoop a little water onto Special she heard another noise coming from somewhere below her knees. She lowered her ear to the floor, nudging it against the warped boards. The noise was coming from deep under the floor. It was a moaning sound, like the wind caught in the leaves of a tree. Or squelching, like feet stuck in a bog. There was a clanging too, like prisioners' chains as they shuffled accross a courtyard. Special clung to her fingers, shivering like it had the day they had climbed the tree.

"We're going," she said to Woody, jumping up. "I don't feel right about this place."

As Fern turned towards the doors, she froze in her tracks, her feet sinking deeper into the moss and her heart skipping a couple of beats.

The great wooden door was opening. Someone was coming into the room.

Fern, Woody and Special dived behind the base of the fountain, landing with a *thud*. Fern peeked above the rim as the botanist from the plane glided into the room. She wore a white lab coat and beneath it Fern could see a sliver of pale skirt. A shimmery scarf was twisted around her head like a bonnet, tied in a sharp knot at the nape of her neck.

"Is that you I heard, Ginkgo? What are you doing in the old ballroom? I have finished my green juice and I'm heading to the roof to feed the parent plants. I trust you have the plant potion ready."

When no one answered, her eyes narrowed and scanned the room like green lasers. "It must be those pesky rats again."

She turned and strode from the room, her lab coat floating behind her like a veil.

Fern stood and started to follow her, as if her body acted without her brain. Woody clutched her arm and yanked her back. "What are you doing?"

"You heard what she said, it's feeding time. Special needs food, so our timing couldn't be more perfect. We don't want to lose her."

He fell in step behind her but Fern could tell he wasn't happy. There was a flash of white ahead as the botanist turned down a corridor, and then through another doorway, and they found themselves at the base of a thin iron staircase.

Fern pointed down at his feet. "Take your shoes off," she whispered. Woody looked at her as if she was mad. "We need to make as little noise as possible."

"No way, my shoes stay on. No shoes, no Woody."

"Then walk on the front of your foot first, then the back."

"That's the wrong way round."

"I know, but it's quieter. We used to walk like that on plant-hunting trips so we didn't disturb the wildlife."

The thin iron staircase took them out of the building, curved around and around itself like a snail's shell, and then delivered them into a rooftop glasshouse. Metal girders ran up its sides like the spine of an enormous see-through beetle. As far and as high as their eyes could see, the space was filled with green.

Fern gasped. It was like being back in the rainforest.

As they stepped forwards, they parted a cloud of coloured butterflies which scattered like tiny pieces of torn paper being blown in the wind. A warm, figgy smell wrapped itself around her nostrils, sweet and delicious.

"This place is beautiful."

"It smells," Woody pinched his nose tightly.

"Like the Amazon and the mountains and meadows all in one," Fern said in wonder. "A garden in the sky."

"There are … so many plants, Fern." Woody was frozen to the spot, as if his feet had been set in concrete, and he was beginning to breathe in and out very quickly, and his face paled. "I should have brought my bag."

"You have your bag, it's on your back." She pointed at his backpack.

"Not that one – my paper bag. When I start to feel a panic attack coming, I breathe into it and it helps. I … I need it, Fern."

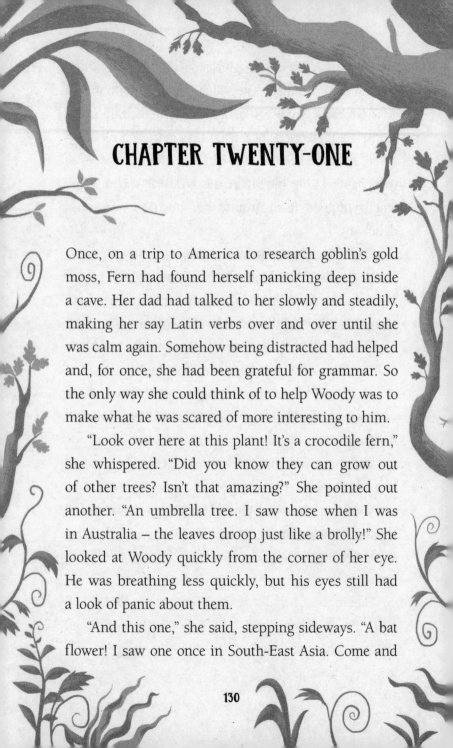

CHAPTER TWENTY-ONE

Once, on a trip to America to research goblin's gold moss, Fern had found herself panicking deep inside a cave. Her dad had talked to her slowly and steadily, making her say Latin verbs over and over until she was calm again. Somehow being distracted had helped and, for once, she had been grateful for grammar. So the only way she could think of to help Woody was to make what he was scared of more interesting to him.

"Look over here at this plant! It's a crocodile fern," she whispered. "Did you know they can grow out of other trees? Isn't that amazing?" She pointed out another. "An umbrella tree. I saw those when I was in Australia – the leaves droop just like a brolly!" She looked at Woody quickly from the corner of her eye. He was breathing less quickly, but his eyes still had a look of panic about them.

"And this one," she said, stepping sideways. "A bat flower! I saw one once in South-East Asia. Come and see. Doesn't it look *exactly* like a bat?" She pressed her finger on the top of the flower so that it moved as if it were flapping its wings.

Ever so slowly, Woody inched towards her, his eyes focused on the flower. It had thin shiny 'wings' and little strands growing out of it like whiskers. He got as near as he dared and then stopped.

"I'm sorry," he said. "I know I should be braver. Especially when I'm the boy," he said.

"Who ever said that boys should be especially brave?" said Fern.

"Everyone thinks they should," said Woody.

"That's *nonsense*," said Fern. "Girls are *just* as brave as boys, and boys are just as un-brave as girls. None of us are brave all the time. I'll tell you a secret. I felt a bit like you do now on the Underground. Small spaces and darkness make me feel dizzy, like I might faint." She could have added that she felt even more weird when she had seen the eerie roots that were growing along the tunnels, but she didn't think that was something Woody needed to hear in this moment.

There was a flash of colour above them as a green parakeet flew past.

"There are animals in here too?" said Woody. "I don't like them much either." His face looked panicked again and his hand shot to his mouth.

"Only up above – they're much too high to bother you!"

At first Fern couldn't tell if Woody was behind her, but as she ducked below a low branch, she smiled as she heard his footsteps following her into the green.

With the soft feeling of the soil gathering between her toes, and her desert hat on her head, Fern soon had a sense of home she hadn't felt since she'd left her parents. She wouldn't have been surprised to hear her dad's voice from ahead shouting, "Ant nest at three o'clock! Mind your ankles, team."

Green wasn't the only colour – there was cobalt blue, sunny yellow and fiery red. On some of the plants there were flowers blossoming, while on others, buds waited patiently for their moment.

Fern pulled up next to a bushy shrub with trumpet-like flowers.

"Don't touch it," she said quickly, putting her arm between the plant and Woody.

"As if I was going to! But it is beautiful," he said, despite himself.

"Beauty isn't always a good thing. Especially in the plant world. Look." Fern pointed at a wooden sign nestled in the soil, painted black with a red skull and crossbones.

"What does that mean?"

"Poison."

Woody jumped back as if he had been stung. "What on earth is she doing with poisonous pla—"

A noise came then, from their left, and Woody dropped his voice to a whisper. "That doesn't sound like a parakeet."

"More like footsteps," said Fern. "Quick, in here," she said, pulling him under the cover of a clump of pampas.

A white wellington boot appeared through the undergrowth, followed by a body covered in white overalls. It was Ginkgo. His face was shrouded in a net, but there was no mistaking his short, squat shape. He carried a spray gun, and as they watched he pressed the trigger and a clear liquid squirted into the air and then misted down onto the plants.

Fern felt a sprinkle land on her hand. Lifting it to her nose cautiously, she sniffed. It was just water.

Work finished, Ginkgo moved off, hitching the spray gun onto his shoulder like a soldier searching out a battle. Fern let out a long, low breath.

Pulling Special out of her bag, she sat the plant on her lap and rocked the teapot back and forth gently in her hands. "Not long now, I promise. We will find something to help you." Special still seemed terrified, which surprised her. Fern had thought it would like being somewhere so green and beautiful.

There was a rustling noise in the grass and a lizard scuttled over Fern's foot. She hoped Woody hadn't seen it.

"Let's keep going. The sooner we can get out of here, the better."

CHAPTER TWENTY-TWO

Deeper and deeper they went, creeping into the crevices between the plants, checking before they crossed an open space and then running quickly to where they could take cover again. There was no sign of the botanist.

Fern was so busy inside her own head that at first she didn't notice the faded wooden cabin emerging between two trees. Its roof was covered in weeds as if it had green punk hair, and a clear pipe poked out from it and disappeared through the wall of the glasshouse. A dark liquid ran through it, rich blood red. Fern wondered where the pipe went to.

"I think I might have found something," she said as Woody caught her up. "Hide behind one of those bushes and keep watch. I'll look inside. If Ginkgo comes back, whistle to warn me. You can whistle, can't you?"

"Of course I can whistle!" Woody looked indignant. "But if they hear me whistle then they'll know where we are, won't they?"

"I suppose so." She hadn't considered that. "What about squawking like a parakeet?"

"I don't have much experience of squawking," said Woody. "It's not the type of thing you learn in school."

"Hissing like a snake, then? That's an easy one." Woody looked at her as if she had gone mad. "I hope there aren't any snakes in here!"

"You'll think of something. I'll be back as soon as I can."

The door of the cabin squeaked gently as she pushed it open. It was dark and musty inside and only the bright sunlight shining in from the glasshouse behind her lit the space a little.

Fern jumped when she saw a line of grey shadowy figures along the wall. She dug her hand into her bag and scrabbled around until she felt the shape of her torch. The thin shard of light from it showed that the shapes were actually large dustbins, lined up like soldiers waiting for inspection. On the front of each one was written what she thought might be a chemical formula: a jumble of letters and numbers that meant nothing to her. Opening the first lid, she found a bright green powder. She opened the second and found white granules, and then a third which smelled peaty and rich.

"There are so many different foods, how do I know which one is right for you?" She lifted a few more lids and then went back to the first, banging her head against something hanging from the ceiling. Her torch revealed a row of hooks from which hung instruments – scoops, sieves and wooden spoons that would not have looked out of place in a giant's kitchen. At the end, on a slim hook, was a fat knife – glinting icicle-sharp in the torch light. Tiptoeing forward, so that she didn't bang into anything else, she saw a chest freezer in the corner. Mist rose from the cracks around its lid like tendrils of smoke from a fire. What could be inside?

Letting her torch lead the way, she saw that to the left of the freezer was a huge glass vat, and inside it a whisk was churning a dark, frothing liquid. Bubbles rose furiously from the bottom and popped at the top, letting out an awful smell. She put her hand to her mouth. It stank!

The clear pipe she had seen from the outside was attached to the top of the vat, and below it was a stack of empty glass bottles. She picked one out. There was a label stuck to the side, and she reached for her magnifying glass so she could make out what it said: *DH Food.* What could that mean? What was DH?

Her plant-hunting bag began to wiggle against her hip. Looking down, she saw Special's tendril poking out of the corner of the bag and pointing towards the vat of dark gunky liquid.

"Is this the one you want? The stinky one? Are you sure?" The tendril flapped surprisingly vigorously. "Let's give that one a go, then, shall we?"

She wedged the bottle to a tap at the side of the vat – the spout of the pipe fitted perfectly inside the glass rim as if they were made for each other. Nothing happened for a moment, but then the strange, dark liquid began to trickle out. As it grew heavier and heavier, she had to put her torch between her teeth and hold it with two hands. Then she almost dropped it after hearing a noise outside.

"Ginkgo!"

The botanist's voice was shrill, as if she was calling a disobedient dog. Why hadn't Woody warned her? She switched the torch and tap off and stood in the dark, her body rattling with fear, clutching the warm bottle to her like a hot water bottle on a cold night.

There was the sound of approaching wellingtons.

"Sorry, ma'am. I was drawing up a *Grapevine* advert to find a new gardener."

"Most clumsy of the last one to die, wasn't it? Still, it's an indication that our project is heading in the right direction. I trust you mentioned nothing about our ambitions?"

"No, ma'am. I wrote merely that we needed someone with good botanical knowledge who was willing to work hard."

"Good, Ginkgo. You must find someone soon. Anyone will do – old or young. We cannot be without help. There is too much to do and a short time to do it in. Did you get more … ingredients?"

"Indeed, ma'am."

Fern inched towards the door and peered through the shard of light above the hinge. She was so close that she could see the botanist's feet; her toes, poking from the end of her sandals, were surprisingly green-looking as if she had been walking through a wet garden.

"Oh, and, Ginkgo?" The botanist turned to look at him and Fern saw her eyes attach themselves to his – unblinking like a lizard. "The search for the lost prototype. Have you made any progress?"

"I have, ma'am. I have contacted the airline. I have checked the crates ten times. It appears that the prototype has disappeared."

"That plant was the result of years of hard work, numerous experiments and a pinch of…"

Fern didn't catch the botanist's last word as she had turned away, eyes following a bat that had skimmed over the top of her head. When she turned back Fern heard her say, "It has broken my heart to have mislaid it."

The botanist must love Special as much as she did. As they walked away, Fern felt so awful she almost rushed out of the cabin to say she could have it back. But something held her back – Special's tendril had slipped from her bag and wrapped itself tightly around her arm, as if in warning.

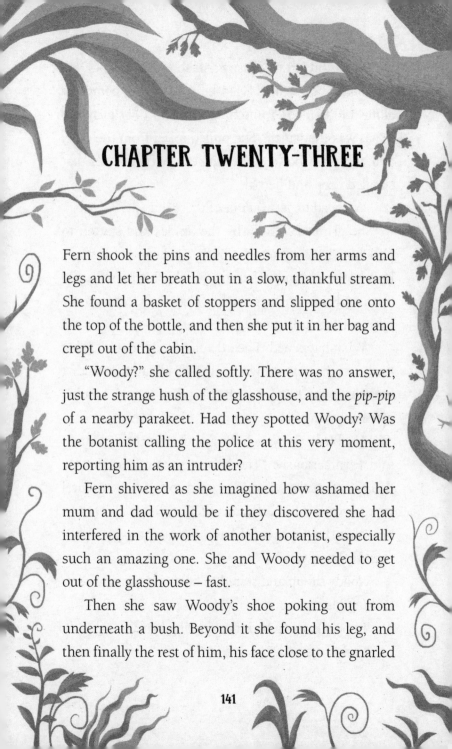

CHAPTER TWENTY-THREE

Fern shook the pins and needles from her arms and legs and let her breath out in a slow, thankful stream. She found a basket of stoppers and slipped one onto the top of the bottle, and then she put it in her bag and crept out of the cabin.

"Woody?" she called softly. There was no answer, just the strange hush of the glasshouse, and the *pip-pip* of a nearby parakeet. Had they spotted Woody? Was the botanist calling the police at this very moment, reporting him as an intruder?

Fern shivered as she imagined how ashamed her mum and dad would be if they discovered she had interfered in the work of another botanist, especially such an amazing one. She and Woody needed to get out of the glasshouse – fast.

Then she saw Woody's shoe poking out from underneath a bush. Beyond it she found his leg, and then finally the rest of him, his face close to the gnarled

141

trunk. His breath was raspy and short. Fern shook his knees and he groaned. Had he panicked at being left alone and fainted? Something tinkled in her memory. What was that smell? She pulled a leaf from the bush and rubbed it between her fingers, releasing oils that smelled deep and herbal.

"We need to get you out of there quickly."

She gripped Woody by the ankles and started to pull him from under the bush. He was surprisingly heavy for someone so skinny. Finally, his eyes flipped open and seemed surprised to find Fern leaning over him, her face full of concern.

"What happened? I heard voices so I hid under that bush and the next thing I knew I felt all faint. I couldn't breathe. It was like I was choking even though I hadn't eaten anything."

"The bush you were hiding under is a cherry laurel," said Fern seriously. "The leaves contain cyanide! My dad said that the Victorians used to put bits of laurel in a jar with a butterfly to watch it die. It's so hot in here that the leaves must have given off the gas and it overwhelmed you."

Woody sat up and stared in horror at the innocent-looking plant.

"I knew it was a bad idea coming here."

"Can you stand?"

Soon he was upright, if a little wobbly. But Fern, usually a good pathfinder through the wild, had lost her bearings. Which way had they come?

They started to thread their way back through the maze-like glasshouse. After five minutes, Woody stopped.

"I think we've passed that orange tree three times," he said. "Do you think we might be going in circles, Fern?"

She hated to admit that she had got them lost. She went to the base of a large feathery tree fern, put her arms around its hairy trunk and began to climb, toes clinging to the gaps in its coarse trunk. As she inched higher and higher towards the glass ceiling, she could see the entire glasshouse below her like a patchwork green quilt. But there was no time to admire the view; the botanist or Ginkgo could be back at any moment. And it was so hot up here near the glass roof that sweat slid off every part of her.

She spotted the opening to the staircase and traced a path to it with her finger, then began to climb down again. Her feet had just touched earth, and she raised her hand to gesture at Woody to follow her, when she felt a violent tug on her hair.

"And who do we have here?"

Ginkgo's face appeared far too close to her own.

Her whole scalp seared in pain as his grip on her hair got tighter.

"I know you," he said. "You were on the plane."

Fern's eyes were stinging like poison had been dropped into them. She yanked her head sideways and pulled free, a few of her hairs staying behind in Ginkgo's hand. Then she ran, pulling Woody after her.

Ginkgo's breath was behind them, laboured but determined. Fern felt the red burn of a stitch starting.

"Woody!" she gasped, clutching at the seed of an idea. "When I say so you have to put your hand over your mouth."

"Why?"

"I haven't got time to explain, just do it!" She turned a sharp left and they came into a clearing. Ahead of them rose a plant so strange and so large that it looked like a giant's pot plant. From within its core grew an enormous white spathe, surrounded by a flower that looked like it was wearing a burgundy ballet tutu.

"Hands!" Fern shouted.

There was the sound of swearing from behind as Ginkgo pulled level with them. His waistcoat was ripped and bits of branch were caught in his hair. As his hands shot out to grab Fern, he managed to catch the strap of her plant-hunting bag and it opened, spilling all of her things onto the ground. Poor Special was tipped upside down and nearly lost all its soil, but held onto the strap for dear life.

"Come here, you—" Ginkgo snarled, but then he broke off and his face seemed to melt like wet wax. He bent over, as if someone had karate-chopped him in the stomach, and there was the sound of retching.

Scooping up Special and the bottle of plant potion, and hoping she hadn't missed anything else, Fern hoisted her bag on her shoulder and they ran out of the glasshouse, down the steps, across the lobby and away from the Magnolia Hotel.

CHAPTER TWENTY-FOUR

"Get on a bus, any bus!" said Woody, and they flung themselves at the first one they saw, climbing to the top seats and sinking into them in relief. Fern looked out of the window, dreading seeing a flash of waistcoat below them, but as the bus trundled through the streets and the botanist's assistant didn't appear, she began to relax.

Woody looked around to check that no one could hear them, then he leaned towards her and whispered, "What happened in there? What was that plant?"

"A corpse plant," said Fern. "I first met one in Indonesia."

"*Corpse* plant?" Woody's eyes widened.

"Nothing to do with real corpses. It got its name because it smells so awful. I've never seen an open one before, I couldn't believe it when I saw it from the top of that tree fern. Did you see the spathe? That's the strange spear bit sticking out of the top of it. It lets out an awful smell that attracts pollinators."

"Pollinators?"

"Insects. Ones that feed on dead animals. They love the corpse plant. It smells revolting and that was why Ginkgo was so sick. Corpse plants only open every seven years, so you have to get very lucky to smell one – or unlucky, maybe. I don't feel very sorry for Ginkgo, though!" She rubbed the raw spot on her scalp where her hair had been tugged.

Woody digested this. "For someone who doesn't like to make plans, that was quite a good one. I'm sorry we didn't find anything to help your plant."

"Didn't we?" Fern raised her eyebrows and smiled.

"What do you mean?"

She dug into her bag and took out the bottle, holding it up to the light so that the scarlet liquid gleamed. "I think this might be just what Special needs – some kind of super-stinky plant food. Whatever important work the botanist is doing, this must be part of what she feeds her plants. She's amazing, isn't she?"

"That isn't the word I would use to describe her. I think she's –" Woody scrambled around to find the right words – "a bit terrifying."

Fern made a cross face at him. "She's just clever. People are always scared of clever, important women –

that's what my mum says. If I knew I could be like her one day then maybe I *would* study hard and become a botanist."

"So you are sure she isn't doing anything bad?" said Woody, still unconvinced. "Why is the glasshouse so secretive?"

"Botanists don't do bad things," said Fern. "They help the world. Plants are our past and our future, and botanists are the people who know about plants." Hearing herself say it like this, Fern wondered whether she was silly not to want to be a botanist one day.

She took Special out of her bag carefully and sat it on her lap.

"I think it must be you she's missing so much," she said guiltily.

"Why are you talking to it?" Woody looked at her as if she was mad.

"Because it understands me," she said. "If it wasn't so poorly I would show you some of its tricks."

"Plants can't do tricks. What language are you even speaking to it? Plant language?" he laughed, though not unkindly.

"I don't speak anything different but Special understands. I always knew that plants understood more than people think… Special is just the proof."

"You're … not very normal, do you know that, Fern?"

"Normal? I don't think you fit in that category either, Woody."

An old man with a small black dog sat in the seat in front of them. The dog stuck its head over the back of the seat and sniffed the air around them, whining a little as if confused by the strange smell coming from the bottle in Fern's bag.

Without warning, the bus veered to the left and the dog landed with a yelp on the floor. Fern saw a giant monkey puzzle tree growing out of the road. Cars were swerving to avoid its spiky branches, drivers honking their horns angrily. Tourists were stood in groups taking photos from a safe distance. In the excitement of saving Special, Fern had forgotten about the giant plants.

Three buses later and she and Woody were walking down Dandelion Road, elbows occasionally brushing. They stopped outside Woody's door and Fern put her hand on his arm and he didn't even flinch.

"Thank you. For coming with me. For being brave. And for not leaving when you found out I'm a thief," said Fern.

"Life has got more complicated since you've been around." Woody grasped his button and spun it gently. "But you're welcome."

One of the front windows was ajar and the sounds of his brothers spilled into the quiet of the early evening. He turned to look at her.

"Let me know how Special does, will you? I hope it feels better soon."

Fern grinned from ear to ear.

"Are you suggesting that it might have feelings, Woody?"

CHAPTER TWENTY-FIVE

Fern took the plant from her bag and placed it on her bedroom floor, gently unwrapping the flannel.

"Oh, Special, you look even worse than you did before." The ends of the plant's tendrils were shrivelling in on themselves and the pod was becoming brown and crispy at the edges.

She took out the bottle of plant food. How much should she pour? The cork made a *pop* as she drew it out, and the liquid fizzed up towards the rim. She pulled Special's teapot nearer, and looked at her limp friend.

"How do I know how much to give you to make you better?" She tilted the bottle towards the plant but then stopped. "I don't want to get it wrong," she said anxiously.

Fern shut her eyes and tried to dig into her memory. She could see her dad on his knees, bent over one of his finds; the tall man at his most gentle, using a medical syringe to drop food onto a plant. She was so clumsy, how was she going to pour such small amounts? It wouldn't do to try and use her toothbrush mug or she might drown it.

"Uncle Ned's burnt chicken!"

She jumped up, almost knocking the bottle over. A few days before, trying to venture beyond toast, Uncle Ned had decided to cook them a small roast chicken. It had been a complete disaster that had led to a burnt bird, a smoky kitchen – and cheese on toast. But before he had turned the unfortunate chicken to charcoal, he had used a baster – it was the perfect thing for making sure that she gave Special only a small amount of the formula.

Fern crept quietly into the kitchen, not wanting to explain what she was doing, but she needn't have worried. Uncle Ned was out in the garden, wearing the full suit of armour, and waving his sword rather feebly at the back wall. She found the baster nestled among a collection of odd forks, a medieval knuckle duster and a chopstick, and crept back upstairs.

"How many drops?" she said to herself when she was in her bedroom. Too much might frazzle Special, yet too little and it might not recover quickly enough and die anyway. She gulped back the thought that she might never play catch-a-fly with it again, or feel its tendrils wrap around her finger. Then she plunged the pipe of the baster into the bottle and squeezed the rubber ball.

The formula crept up the baster, and with her hand trembling, Fern inserted the glass tip into the soil, took a deep breath and squeezed softly. Once, twice, three times. She stopped. Three felt like a good number. She picked the plant up and placed it gently beside her bed. She didn't know what she could do now, apart from wait and hope. Wrapping herself in her duvet like a sausage roll, she shut her eyes.

There was the sound of bells chiming from downstairs and a news announcer's voice, which was so serious it sounded like he was gargling gravel.

"Good evening, London. Buckingham Palace has announced that the Royal Family has been evacuated to Windsor Castle after a colossal trumpet lily invaded the palace. The family were removed an hour ago, after a shoot of the plant grew through the smallest prince's bedroom window, whereupon he woke and alerted a member of staff.

"The young princess, who is a keen gardener, was found by her eldest brother trying to take a soft cutting from the plant, which has now been removed and is being held as police evidence. The palace is cordoned off and a team from Kew Gardens is due on the scene to open investigations."

Fern's eyes popped open in surprise. Uncle Ned must have left the radio on in the kitchen and the noise was meandering up the stairs. Closing her eyes again, she fell asleep hoping that the news wasn't on in the house next door.

When she woke next morning, a fly was investigating Fern's nose. Then it took a walk across her cheek. She flung her fingers up to swat it away and found something long and stringy instead of something with wings. She sat up sharply.

"Special! Are you back?!"

From the way that its pod was shaking she was sure that the plant was laughing. Where it had been droopy, now it was upright. Where it had been a dull colour, there was shine again.

Looking at her plant, a small part of her wondered if she was still asleep and dreaming. Everything else was still the same size: her floor-bed, the rug, the strange picture on the wall of the lady with the flouncy dress. It was only Special that was bigger. Quite a *lot* bigger. The day before, its pod had been the size of a golf ball, now it was the size of an orange. Its stem was as fat as a sink pipe and its coiled leaves the size of Roman snails. It had outgrown the teapot completely.

"Did I sleep for a *month* or something?"

Special shook its pod and pointed at the plant potion, which was bubbling away on the shelf in the corner.

"So it didn't just make you better, it made you grow. I'd better not give you too much or you won't fit in the house soon!" Special shook its pod and pointed at the plant potion again.

"You want some more? Just a tiny bit, then." She trickled a little more onto the soil. "That's enough." But when she stopped, Special tried to grab the bottle and she had to push it away. It threw itself forward in a sulk and started bashing its tendrils on her arm.

"Don't have a tantrum!" Fern patted its pod with a finger to try and calm it down. "You must really like it, eh?" It was hard to understand how it could like something that smelled quite so disgusting. She put the bottle safely out of its reach. "It's for your own good, I'm sure Bert Beetle wouldn't advise me to feed you *every* day."

Special tilted its pod as if to say that Bert Beetle would definitely advise her to feed it every day.

"Besides, I don't want to have to see Ginkgo any time soon, I had a dream last night that I was running away from him but my legs wouldn't move. Come on, we're going downstairs, away from temptation." She picked the teapot up, groaning at how heavy it was. "I'm going to have to get you another pot somehow, this one is going to break under your weight. But first we've got someone to go and see!"

Fern couldn't get round to Woody's quickly enough. That was what you did when you had a friend, wasn't it? As soon as you had good news or bad news, you told them first.

She knocked on the door, but there was no answer. She knocked again. Still no answer. As she turned to leave she saw the twitching of a curtain in an upstairs window, and felt sure she saw Woody's face.

She walked home much more slowly.

CHAPTER TWENTY-SIX

A week later and there was no stopping Special; it had a pod like a small melon and its spike was like a crocheting needle.

"Don't grow any bigger or you could really hurt someone with that," Fern said. Special turned away sheepishly. "It's all right, I don't mind. I still love you even if you are turning into a pin cushion."

Fern began to keep a chart of Special's growth, measuring its height and width each morning. They had daily walks to the park for fresh air and tree climbing. The bigger it got, the harder it was to hide from Uncle Ned, so she would wait until she heard snores from his room before hurrying down the stairs and out into the world – and sneak back upstairs while he was busy singeing their toast.

She spotted Woody at the park a few times, but when she called his name, he would disappear quickly into his house. She couldn't understand it. Were friendships a bit like seedlings and some of them just didn't survive past the first tiny bit of growth?

Now that Special was well again, and now that she seemed to have lost Woody for reasons she couldn't explain, Fern turned once again to her running-away plan.

If she was going to fly, she needed money, much more than her pocket money (which was just coins, never notes). The only way she could think of to get money, since she didn't have anything worth selling, was to get a job. The problem was, she had no idea how to go about getting one of those.

So she took her sketchbook out from under her floor bed once again and wrote a list of what she was good at, which was difficult because she couldn't think of much, but also because Special kept stealing her pencil. Snatching it back, she used the rubber end to give it a quick tickle, which made it shake all over. If only there was some kind of job where you got to be with plants all day, she'd be good at that...

An idea sprang into her head.

Ginkgo had said that the botanist was going to need someone to work as a gardener. Was it crazy to think that she might apply? She had hardly been able to stop thinking about the botanist since they had escaped, and although Ginkgo still terrified her, if there was some way of impressing the botanist, perhaps he wouldn't matter. She had seemed desperate, after all. *Anyone will do, young or old. As long as they have good botanical knowledge and are willing to work hard.* Could it really be that hard to be a gardener?

She looked at Special. It was so big now, there was no way she could hide it in her dungarees pocket or even in her plant-hunting bag to go on a plane. It might even need an extra seat, and how much would *that* cost? Two tickets to Africa would mean she needed to save up more than she had first thought. She stood up. She was wasting time sitting and worrying. This was the only plan she could think of, so it was time to do something about it.

Fern lay Bert Beetle's book flat on the floor, took a deep breath, and began to study. Every time she felt a flicker of protest from her restless feet she ignored them, and when her hands began to fidget with boredom, she sat on them. Every time she wanted to give up and go outside to play, she carried on. Bert's beautiful pictures willed her onwards, and his words were slipping into her memory – and staying put.

She wrote the Latin names for plants, and she drew sketches of them and made lists of the chemicals found in them. Soon there were scraps of paper scattered around her like fallen petals. If she was going to try and get a job with a world-famous botanist, she needed to prove to her that she knew everything there was to know about plants.

After a few hours had ticked past, Fern came across a chapter she found especially interesting. After taking some careful notes and looking very, very closely at Special, she shut her botany book and smiled.

"I think I know what you are!" she said, surprising even herself. "You aren't one plant, you are *three*."

She picked up three pieces of paper and held them in front of her and read aloud:

"*Barrel cactus: a rare cactus with sharp spikes. Strangling fig: an air plant that becomes a parasite. Venus flytrap: a carnivorous plant that preys on insects.* You have bits of all of these plants! I wonder why the botanist has created you from all of them?"

There was a soft knock on the door and she startled, looking around at the mess of paper all over the room. Thinking quickly, she threw her duvet over Special.

"I have something for you," Uncle Ned said.

He was holding a long, thin box, which he handed her sheepishly. Inside there was cream tissue paper, and beneath that, a pair of shiny leather shoes.

"I am afraid that they won't understand your preference to be without shoes once you start at school. Schools are not really barefoot kinds of places."

Fern had almost forgotten that Uncle Ned had registered her for the school at the end of the road. It was not long until the new term started.

She knew that when someone gave you a gift you had to look very grateful indeed, even if it was the last thing in the world you wanted. Slipping each foot in, Fern braced herself as she felt the cool slide of the leather.

They felt stiff and unwelcoming. She bent over and fastened the laces, then stood up, trying not to show Uncle Ned how uncomfortable they felt.

"Try walking in them!" he said enthusiastically. She stepped cautiously along the uneven floor, the shoes squeaking like little mice. She would never be able to run in these and certainly not climb.

"You will have to wear them in – there is nothing worse than blisters on your first day of school. I suggest wearing them every day from now until the new term begins next week."

Uncle Ned had a funny expression on his face as he gazed at her. It took Fern a little while to realize that it was pride. He gave her an awkward hug, the first he had ever given her, and then turned to walk out the door.

There was a flash of green and suddenly Special's tendril had snuck out from under the duvet and grabbed his trousered leg.

"Ouch!" Uncle Ned startled.

That made Special squeeze even harder. Fern picked up her pencil and stabbed it at the duvet. The tendril let go and sprang back beneath the duvet sulkily. Luckily, Uncle Ned's glasses were only just hanging on to the end of his nose, which meant he hadn't seen a thing.

"What was *that*?" he gasped.

"It was me," she said. "Sorry."

"What on earth were you thinking, Fern?"

"Sorry, Uncle Ned, I really am. I don't know what came over me."

"Is it the shoes? Don't you like them?"

"No, the shoes are lovely. Really lovely, thank you, Uncle Ned." It wasn't exactly a lie, because she could see that they were a lovely pair of shoes. They just weren't shoes that she would ever feel happy in.

"You naughty plant! You were jealous, weren't you?" she said when he had gone. "You were jealous of him giving me a hug."

Special shook its pod defiantly.

"You have to be careful. If he realizes I have you, he might take you away. I'm going to the park now, and I'm leaving you here as punishment. All on your own." The plant turned its pod away from her moodily.

As she swung the gate open, she saw Woody hurrying along the pavement with his head down, overflowing bags of shopping in each hand.

CHAPTER TWENTY-SEVEN

"Woody!" she called, dashing down the street towards him. "You should see Special! It's so healthy and growing more and more every day. The plant potion worked! It's becoming quite naughty, though, it doesn't just catch flies now – it catches beetles and butterflies and—"

Fern stopped talking as Woody tried to slip past her.

"Is something the matter?" His eyes looked set, and he wasn't smiling back at her.

"Will you come round soon?" she said. "You could come and see Special, maybe bring a jigsaw? We could do it together." If she hoped that would win him over, she was wrong. He was walking away even quicker now.

"I can show you how Special catches tennis balls. I've moved it on from marbles now as it's so big."

Woody finally stopped although he didn't turn around.

"I haven't got time for silly girls and stupid plants," he said.

"But I thought…" Could she say this? She didn't know, but she was going to anyway. "I thought we were becoming friends."

"I never said that." He spun around and his eyes were hard. It didn't suit them.

"Have I done something wrong?"

"Juniper hurt himself while we were out on that stupid adventure of yours. He fell off a chair and bumped his head really badly and Ajee had to spend the whole day in the hospital with him and the other two."

"Is he … is he OK?" She was relieved when he nodded.

"She's not as young as she was, she can't be in three different places at once watching them, they move really quickly now and they have a terrible taste for trouble. Ajee feels really bad that he hurt himself, but it was my fault." He started walking up the street again. "It's a hard time for all of my adults right now and I should never have left Ajee and come with you."

"I'm sorry, Woody," Fern said. "I wouldn't want anything bad to happen to any of your brothers. But … just five minutes? Please? I would love you to come." It was important to be honest with friends about what you were feeling, wasn't it?

Woody shook his head stubbornly.

"I promised my dad, and I'm not going to break that promise again. I don't have time for messing around like you do, Fern. Please, just leave me alone." He was outside his house now – she had followed him all the way along the street and he ran up the path before she could say anything more. Even the door closing behind him sounded unfriendly.

Fern felt a painful jab somewhere around her middle. It was almost worse to think you had a sort-of friend and then lose them than to never have had one in the first place. Plants, Fern decided (not for the first time), were much easier than people, even if hers had a bit of a jealousy problem.

When Fern got home, Uncle Ned was thrumming around the kitchen.

"Pilchards are underrated, you know," he said, catching a piece of toast as it flung itself from the toaster. "They are especially good on toast as the salty juice seeps down into the bread. You must try some. I find a little raw onion sets it off perfectly."

Fern reached quickly for the lemon curd before he had a chance to put one of the tiny fish on her slice of toast.

After tea Uncle Ned said, "You seem a little quiet, Fern, I trust that everything is all right?"

Fern said nothing. Uncle Ned changed tack.

"We should make the most of this weather – they say there are more storms coming in. Really the weather is quite peculiar here, it seems to get wetter each summer."

"Woody doesn't want to play with me," Fern blurted out.

Uncle Ned was not particularly in tune with the minds of young children, but as an author he was used to watching people's faces, and the one he saw in front of him now held a few signs that made him concerned.

"Let us do something together, then. Just the two of us," he said. "We'll go to one of the great parks! They all have their merits: Kensington Gardens has Peter Pan; Hyde Park has a fountain; and Regent's Park has its roses. But tomorrow, I feel, will be a St James's day. We'll go and see the pelicans. I am ever so partial to a pelican." He looked like a small boy who had been told he was to have a great treat.

"Are there really pelicans in London?" said Fern, surprised out of her gloom for a moment.

"Well, of course there are. Very fine ones too."

"London doesn't seem a very pelican kind of a place, that's all."

"The longer you live here, the more you will find that London is full of surprises," said Ned. "And you –"

he jabbed his buttery knife at the manuscript beside him – "Sir Garridan, will be staying right here. No parks for you, you would cause untold trouble. This is a trip for me and my niece."

CHAPTER TWENTY-EIGHT

"I think I will have to leave you here."

Special turned away from Fern grumpily.

"You are getting so big now I could hardly carry you in my bag. Besides, Uncle Ned has said he is going to leave Garridan behind, so I think I should leave you behind too."

The plant turned back to her and opened up its tendrils as though it were asking to be picked up.

"Don't make a fuss, you're perfectly well now! You'll be fine here on your own, and tomorrow I'll go back to the Magnolia Hotel and see if the botanist will give me a job in that amazing glasshouse. We'd like to go there every day, wouldn't we?"

Fern swept from the room without a second glance, picking up her new shoes on the way out of the door.

It took her about ten minutes to realize that she loved St James's Park. There really were pelicans, great big ones with beaks like buckets and gazing, watchful eyes.

"I've always felt somewhat of an affinity with pelicans," said Uncle Ned. "Something about their gangly legs and ridiculous noses, I expect."

He pushed his glasses up his own nose and rifled around in his corduroy pockets. "I've brought them a treat. No doubt they are bored with eating those endless pellets. Ah ha!" He pulled out the leftover pilchards Fern had managed to avoid the evening before.

"Are you supposed to do that?" Fern was a little shocked. "There's a sign over there saying not to feed them."

"Is there?" Uncle Ned said, taking his glasses off, putting them in his pocket, and winking at her. "I don't see one."

The pelicans, smelling something delicious, waddled over and nudged each other out of the way to get closer to the man with the fish.

"Did you know there have been pelicans in this very park since 1664?" he said, sitting on a bench and flicking one of the slippery fish towards the largest pelican. "The first ones were a gift from the Russian ambassador to King Charles the Second. History can be quite fascinating when you see it brought to life. The very same type of birds stood here hundreds of years ago, although I suspect they didn't have tinned pilchards then. Here, why don't you have a go?"

Fern flinched as her fingers met with the oily little body, and as the pelicans barged towards her she threw it at them, laughing as they fought over it, giving each other sharp pokes with their beaks. One of them jumped up next to them on the bench and started butting her greedily.

"Oi!" A park warden in a hat appeared and shouted at them. "Stop feeding my birds."

"Perhaps we had better go," said Uncle Ned, emptying the contents of the tin onto the ground. "I fear our speed should be a little faster than my usual gentle ramble." They ran across the park, laughing, the pelicans looking longingly after them.

They stopped to catch their breath beneath a row of large trees.

"I remember coming here with your father many years ago, and him telling me that these trees, London planes, they are called, are one of the greatest hybrids ever created. I always think they are like lines of soldiers with their khaki trunks. Very friendly soldiers, of course. I believe he told me that they are a combination of an American sycamore and an oriental plane tree. Like Londoners, it is their diversity that makes them strong, and these trees actually thrive in the city's pollution. Look, I'll show you what Darwin showed me."

He hopped clumsily over a small metal fence and past a sign saying: *KEEP OFF THE GRASS*, and approached one of the trees, a bigger version of what Fern thought of as her tree in the Dandelion Road park. He pulled off a piece of the bark, which came away as easily as a sticker from its backing.

"Do you think we should being doing that, Uncle Ned?" She wasn't used to someone being more adventurous than her! But he was beckoning her over.

"When the plants are feeling a little too polluted, they just shed a layer. If only we could do that to the planet and start all over again! Isn't botany fascinating?" They hopped back over the fence again and fell into step. Fern smiled as she thought what wonderful company her sign-ignoring uncle could be when he let himself away from his work.

There was a small coffee shop in the middle of the park, and they stopped to buy two cups of hot chocolate. Music came from a speaker and a happy buzz of people paused their walks for something sugary.

"Mmmmmm," said Uncle Ned, taking a large slug from his cup and leaving himself with a foamy moustache. "Cacao. One of the things we can be most grateful to the plant world for."

Fern drank until there was only a slick of dark chocolate left in the bottom of her mug, and when she looked up from it, Uncle Ned's kind eyes were focused on hers from behind his glasses.

"I hope you are not *too* unhappy here, Fern."

She swallowed guiltily. Had he found her running away plan?

"I suspect you must miss them very much – your parents."

"A bit," she said, not wanting to describe the worries she had sometimes in the middle of the night, that her parents might never come and get her, or that something terrible might happen to them and she would never see them again.

"I do understand, you know, a little of how you might be feeling. I was sent away to boarding school when I was young, after our mother died." His face looked sharper at the edges as he spoke. "It wasn't like it is in the books, I can assure you. My school was full of draughty halls and lumpy porridge and at night you could usually hear one of the other boys crying into their pillow because they were so homesick. I got used to it in the end, even enjoyed it for the most part, but those first few months were very difficult. It takes a while to readjust. Not unlike one of your parents' specimens, I would imagine; there is some initial root damage and it takes time to mend again."

Fern wasn't quite able to meet his eyes, but she

shuffled a little closer to Uncle Ned and nodded silently.

"I think I am a little lonely. I thought I had a friend, a real one. I'm not sure I'll find another one." She couldn't mention anything about Special; she was pretty sure uncles didn't understand about such things.

"Friends are to be found in unusual places, Fern. I know Garridan as well as I know any of my real friends. He has been terrifically loyal when I have been going through some of life's more difficult times. Did I tell you he first showed himself to me when he was still a lord's apprentice, not long after my mother died. No? Well, he just appeared one day, his usual insolent self, no explanation as to why he was there. He came to boarding school with me, and his escapades kept me amused when I was at my most unhappy. He hasn't left me since, even though there are times when I wish that he would!"

Fern smiled. She supposed if you could be friends with a plant then maybe you could be friends with someone you'd invented out of a collection of words.

They walked companionably back to the bus stop, feeding the tame squirrels with crumbs from Uncle Ned's pocket.

"I must say it feels rather nice to be awake at a time when things are happening, and not while the rest of the world is asleep. I wish we had done this sooner.

Perhaps from now on our Sundays could be spent exploring London together?"

"I would like that," said Fern, and she meant it. For however many Sundays that would be.

CHAPTER TWENTY-NINE

Uncle Ned fell asleep reading his newspaper on the bus so Fern took out her sketchbook and put it on her lap. She felt more than a little guilty. When she had first decided to run away, there had been no reason to stay here in London. Things felt a little different now.

Ned was kind and thoughtful and, although he was odd, she liked that about him. As she looked out of the bus window, she decided she liked London too. She liked its hustle *and* its bustle; she liked the feeling that there were so many people in this place with so many stories and that each one was different but just as important. There had never been many people in her life – and now she was surrounded by them.

Fern wondered if you could feel two things at once. Could you wish so hard to be back with your parents that it hurt, and at the same time feel that you liked a place and a person very much and would be sad to say goodbye to them?

She had to prod her uncle awake when the bus stopped at the end of Dandelion Road.

"Now, where did I put my key? I really am such a forgetful person." He patted his pockets and turned them out, and eventually found it rolled up in his newspaper.

"Stilton and jam with our toast today, I think. An unusual combination but they will flatter each other as if they are in a choir – a soprano and a baritone in edible harmony."

He reached the key towards the lock. "Oh dear, now look what a silly person I have been."

The front door was ajar.

"I'm sure I locked it. I remember telling Garridan to stay inside as I turned the key and he was in the most dreadful sulk." Uncle Ned scratched his head.

Stepping into the hall, it seemed that the coat rack had finally given in to gravity and the floor was a mound of fallen clothes. In the kitchen, Uncle Ned's pile of papers lay like fresh snowfall across the floor and his bottle of ink had smashed, a splintered glass island in a sea of black ink.

"Oh!" he gasped. "I know I am messy but I don't think I left it looking as bad as this." He stood and looked at his home as if he was watching a boat sinking in front of him. "Oh, Fern, what has happened?" He collapsed onto a chair with a *bump*.

He was so distraught that Fern had to take charge, picking up the papers and sorting them back into a pile.

"What on earth has happened here? What could anyone possibly want from our house? My first editions!" he said suddenly. "Perhaps someone wanted to steal them. One of Garridan's fans, perhaps? They can be a little obsessive."

He rushed upstairs to check, but Fern somehow knew that all his books were exactly where he had left them. Something tugged hard at her guts and wouldn't let go. She also turned to the stairs and climbed them two at a time, flinging open the door of her room.

Even before she looked inside, she knew with horrible clarity exactly what the thief had been after. She knew what valuable thing they wanted. It might not be what other people thought was valuable, but to her it was priceless.

On the floor of her bedroom there was only the trace of a circle where Special's teapot had been, and a small smattering of soil.

Just as Special was getting better, just as everything was less worrying, this had happened. It really was too awful. And it was all her fault. She thought she had lost her key on the string but it must have been in her plant-hunting bag when it was ripped from her shoulder in the glasshouse. And Uncle Ned's address must have been in there too, she always kept that with it because it had her dad's handwriting on it.

It was then that she saw the plant. Stubby, with delicate fan-shaped leaves, it sat on the cardboard box by her bed. It felt as though the thief was still here – an intruder in her safe place, a horrible whisper in the corners of her bedroom. Because Bert Beetle had taught her what this plant was. Older than mankind, this plant had once been a food for dinosaurs.

It was a *ginkgo* plant.

CHAPTER THIRTY

Ginkgo had come for Special, there was no doubt about that. To think he might have been here, watching and waiting for them to go out, was horrible.

She opened the window and searched the street, but there was no sign of him.

"Where did he go? Which way? Tell me," she spun around and shouted crossly at the plant, but it didn't move. This plant wasn't like Special, it couldn't understand her. It was just a normal plant in a pot.

Fern felt a rush of anger surge through her and she swung at the plant, just missing it with her fist. Then, feeling the fury pool down to her feet, she kicked at it. The plant tipped to one side and crashed on the floor.

She looked at it in shock. She had never hurt a plant before. Fern picked it up and put it the right way. It looked a bit battered and a few of the leaves were crushed but she hoped that she hadn't damaged it too badly. "I'm sorry. It isn't your fault that someone so awful is named after you. It's my fault, I should never have left Special alone."

"It sounds like you're entertaining a small herd of elephants," shouted Uncle Ned up the stairs. "I'm just putting a pot of tea on, a dash of brandy for the shock for me, and then I'll call the police to report what's happened."

Fern hardly ate that evening and couldn't sleep. Uncle Ned was writing the final chapters of his book in the kitchen and seemed to have forgotten about the break-in entirely; meanwhile Fern's anger fermented slowly, swaddling her until she felt she couldn't breathe. As the clock across the park struck midnight, she went back to her window and looked out.

"What is it Mum always says?" she said to the moon as there was no one else to hear. "*Don't sit around under a tree waiting for a coconut to fall on your head.* Well, I'm not going to sit around and do nothing. I'll go and get Special back."

But *how* she was going to do it she was less sure about. She wasn't even sure how to get to the Magnolia Hotel again. She couldn't ask Woody, he wanted her to leave him alone. Uncle Ned was busy writing – and it'd mean telling him about Special, which she just didn't think he'd believe, whatever he said about finding friends in strange places.

She had no choice: she would have to go alone.

In the morning, the typewriter was silent and Uncle Ned was asleep with his head on the kitchen table. Peering over his shoulder, Fern saw that the last piece of paper bore only two words: *The End*. He must have finished in the early hours. She felt happy for him, he had worked so hard. She wondered what happened to Garridan when a book was finished – did he have a break too?

She let herself out of the door and stood on Dandelion Road and took a deep breath. How difficult could it be? She had travelled the world; surely she could cross London?

Ten minutes later she stood beneath the red circle of the Underground station. A metal gate barred the entrance, and in front of it was a poster board with a message penned across it that read just like a poem:

Thanks to the Guerrilla Gardener
For making our work so much harder
Another tunnel collapsed last night
Our poor drivers had a solid fright.
Sorry to our passengers, you'll have to walk
(and if you know the gardener, tell him we want to talk?)

Your London Underground team

Fern had not been looking forward to going back beneath London. She had been preparing herself to feel scared again, and had wondered whether she would be able to understand the confusing map. But now that option had been taken away from her, she felt even more worried. The anger she had felt the night before turned to fear. And, without Woody by her side, she felt more than a little lonely.

For a fleeting moment she considered going back to the safety of Dandelion Road. She could wait for Uncle Ned to wake up and they could have a celebratory round of toast.

But as quickly as those comforting thoughts came her way, she pushed them away again. Special was her friend, her only friend. This was all her fault. She might feel scared, but Special must be feeling terrified.

Taking out her compass from her plant-hunting bag, she waited for it to still. Woody had said that the City was to the west, so west she would go.

A voice popped into her head. "Be sensible, Fern, don't let your curiosity run away with you." It was her dad's deep burr, but it was too late to listen to him – her curiosity had already landed her in a heap of trouble. She was just going to have to follow her feet, like she always had.

But an hour later Fern was completely lost. London seemed so much bigger now that she was on her own. She had convinced herself that if she kept walking west she would find something she recognized, but the street signs held names she didn't know and the buses were going to places she had never heard of. It felt like it was her against London – and London was winning. She had been splashed by a bus, almost toppled by a cyclist who'd shouted a rude word at her, and the fumes from the dawdling lines of cars were starting to give her a headache.

She wanted to turn back, but she was so disorientated she couldn't work out which way back *was*. She was hungry, her feet ached and her heart was sinking lower with every step. At last she gave up and sat on the stairs of a red-bricked synagogue and poked her throbbing feet out in front of her. What she would do for a slice of Halo's butter cake.

Fern was not prone to crying, but tears ran down her face anyway, tasting hot and salty on her tongue. She'd lost Special – and now she'd lost herself.

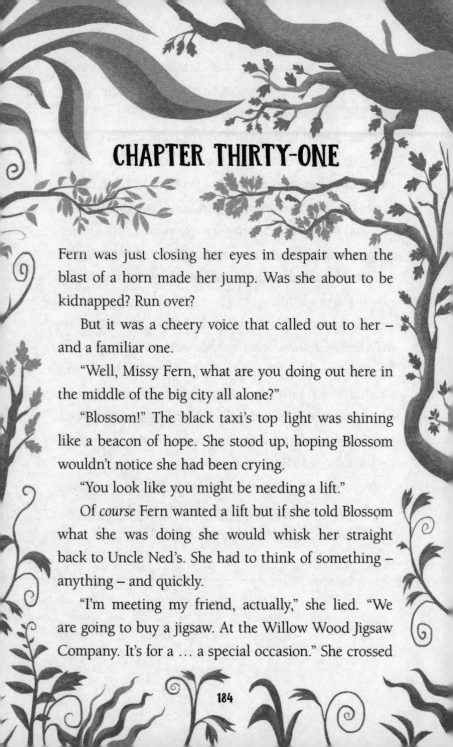

CHAPTER THIRTY-ONE

Fern was just closing her eyes in despair when the blast of a horn made her jump. Was she about to be kidnapped? Run over?

But it was a cheery voice that called out to her – and a familiar one.

"Well, Missy Fern, what are you doing out here in the middle of the big city all alone?"

"Blossom!" The black taxi's top light was shining like a beacon of hope. She stood up, hoping Blossom wouldn't notice she had been crying.

"You look like you might be needing a lift."

Of *course* Fern wanted a lift but if she told Blossom what she was doing she would whisk her straight back to Uncle Ned's. She had to think of something – anything – and quickly.

"I'm meeting my friend, actually," she lied. "We are going to buy a jigsaw. At the Willow Wood Jigsaw Company. It's for a … a special occasion." She crossed her fingers behind her back. Telling yet another lie made her feel queasy, but she wasn't going to give up on her quest to find Special.

"A friend!" bellowed Blossom. "I knew you would find happiness here. But you keep walking this way you will be in France before you are in the City. Come on, hop in with ol' Blossom, let me take you."

"I don't have much money to pay you."

"Ah, don't you worry, little lady. I don't just drive a taxi to be paid, I drive a taxi because of the people I meet, and I like to meet young people like you. Makes ol' Blossom feel young again."

Fern dived into the taxi before she had a chance to change her mind.

"How is London treating you?"

"London is treating me very well, thank you. I like it very much,"

"Didn't I tell you it's the best city in the world? You get bored of London, you get bored of life – that's what I was saying to my Sid last night."

Fern let Blossom's happy chatter run over her like a sprinkler as London flashed past. Seeing the reflection of clouds in the top of a building, she sat up excitedly.

"That's the Shard, isn't it?" Finally, something she recognized.

"Correct!" Blossom's chuckle sounded pleased.

"Quite the Londoner you are already. Look at the window cleaners up there trying to polish it through the leaves. That Guerrilla Gardener sonny, he knows how to make life difficult, don't he? Last night a purple buddleia appeared and swallowed up the BBC building, then bees came from all over London; the noise was like nothing else, they say, couldn't make any programmes. First time there's been no news broadcast since television was invented." For once Blossom's voice sounded a bit serious.

"They're only plants, I suppose – they can't hurt anyone," said Fern.

"Well, Blossom here likes plants as much as the next person, especially ones you can eat. But some of these plants is getting mighty scary. Imagine if that creeper up there grows so big it squeezes the Shard and breaks it – there would be a glass rainstorm a mile wide!" she said, taking her hands off the wheel for a moment to show just how far the glass would fall.

Fern's throat began to throb. The philodendron seemed to have doubled in size since she and Woody had seen it.

Blossom turned the radio on.

"Good morning, London! Mayor Dharma Dahlia is advising Londoners to stay in their homes unless they have

*urgent business. A new scourge of giant plants has appeared
in the centre of the city overnight and there are reports
coming in of a number of people being taken to hospital to
be treated for injuries after an enormous pomegranate fell
from a tree and split, pelleting them with seeds. More news
in an hour."*

Blossom sighed heavily. "What is happening to
our city, eh? If that Guerrilla Gardener messes with
my run-ner beans, I'll be givin' him something I'm
telling you."

As the red door of the Willow Wood factory came
into view, Fern felt her tummy stiffen at the thought
that they were so close to the Magnolia Hotel. Only
now did her courage start to flicker. Was she doing the
right thing? Did Special belong to her at all? And did
she have enough of a plan?

But Blossom was already smoothing the taxi into
a spot right outside and it was too late for second
thoughts.

"I wish I could come and have a gander at the
puzzles, but I'd best be picking up a fare! We can't
exist on air, as my Sid says."

Fern pushed open the stiff taxi door and stepped
onto the waiting pavement.

"Thank you, Blossom."

"Maybe I should wait until your friend comes." There were the faintest crinkles of concern around Blossom's eyes. But a man in a sharply cut suit was walking towards them with his arm thrust in the air. "Paddington!" he snapped, and without waiting for an answer, he slid into the back seat.

"Go careful, missy!" Blossom called as she pulled away.

Fern was alone again.

She mustn't give herself time to think or she might change her mind. Special was all that mattered. She thrust her shoulders back and marched through the door and into the lobby of the Magnolia Hotel.

CHAPTER THIRTY-TWO

Ginkgo was sitting at the front desk. He looked up and, when he saw it was her, his eyes narrowed.

"You," he growled, "have made my life considerably more difficult. What are you doing back here?"

Fern didn't shift her gaze from his; she looked back at him as fiercely as she could.

"I would like to see the botanist," she said, hoping he couldn't hear the tremble in her voice. He folded his newspaper, as neatly and slowly as if it was a piece of origami, and laid it on the desk.

"And why would the greatest botanist in the world want to see a little girl, and a thieving one at that?"

"I'm here for my plant."

He broke into laughter, and it got louder and louder, like a roll of thunder. Then there was the sound of footsteps and a sharp-angled shadow fell over Fern. Ginkgo went quiet. The botanist had appeared at his side, wearing stiff, starched overalls, her hair tied in the calico scarf.

"What *is* going on here?" she purred. Her presence lit up the gloomy lobby as if someone had turned on one of the rusted chandeliers. Fern took a deep breath.

"I was telling your assistant that I'm here for Special. It's my plant and I want it back." She pushed her feet into the ground as if they were roots that could not be moved. Nobody was going to put her off, not even Ginkgo. Although looking at him now, she saw a guilty look on his face. Clearly he had not told the botanist where he had retrieved the plant from, no doubt to cover his own mistake at allowing it to be stolen in the first place. Small indentations appeared in the botanist's cheek as her lips pursed.

"It sounds like I need to have a word with my assistant," she said. "But, please, explain how it can be your plant? Why, you don't even know what that plant is."

"I *do*," Fern said defiantly. "I know exactly what it is. I know you created Special as a hybrid of a barrel cactus, a strangling fig and a Venus flytrap." She stopped and looked at the botanist's face but it was impossible to read, and so she carried on. "I know that it has features of all three of them, but that it's something entirely new and different."

The ghost of a smile flickered on the botanist's lips. "Correct. Three quite magnificent plants in their own right; but combined..." Her eyes took on a dreamy look before they refocused and honed in on Fern. "How sweet that you named it. I must say, it is wonderful to discover such a talented young botanist. I am sure you don't know their scientific names, though?"

"I do," Fern said firmly. "*Echinocactus grusonii, Ficus aurea* and *Dionaea muscipula*." She felt a rush of pride. Her studying had paid off.

"Impressive. I always consider the young to be more interested in the animal world than the plant world. You have surprised me ... and I like to be surprised." The botanist turned and looked towards the lobby entrance as if she was contemplating something, then she turned back again.

"As you have shown yourself to be such a keen scientist, perhaps you might like to come and see a little of my work. I can give you a ... *unique* experience of it."

Little fireworks went off in Fern's brain, melting away any worry that she might have been feeling about Special. She was going to see this amazing, important botanist at work. How proud her parents would be! And once the botanist saw how much she knew, how much she had learned, there was no way that she wouldn't let Fern have Special back.

"Good." She took hold of Fern's chin, tipping her face back gently. "But we haven't been properly introduced. How rude of me. I am Professor Silk, though I am not one for formal names, so you must call me by my first name, Oleander. Yes, I remember you now. You caught my hat that day, at the airport. It was so kind of you. Perhaps you already had my prototype then?"

She looked at Ginkgo, suspicion burning in her eyes, and gently dropped Fern's chin. "Still, we can put that behind us. I'm sure you know that what you did was wrong. This way." The botanist wasn't heading for the stairs, but for a small door at the back of the lobby that Fern hadn't noticed before.

"Let's step outside while it is still dry. Then perhaps later you can play a part in an experiment I am about to bring to its exciting conclusion." Fern fell into her slipstream, following her out of the door.

CHAPTER THIRTY-THREE

The hotel's outside garden was a wild jumble of plants and trees, twisted together like a crocheted blanket. Birds flitted from perch to perch as if it was a playground, and grasshoppers sang from secret hidey holes. The glasshouse had been ordered and organized – but this garden felt like it did what it wanted.

"Welcome to my secret wild," said Oleander, drawing in the fresh air through her nose and letting it out gently through her mouth. "I am never happier than when I am out here. Let's sit on the bench and catch the sun as if we are photosynthesizing." They sat side by side on an old bench with cracked slats.

Fern, suddenly feeling tremendously shy, looked down at her feet. Following her gaze, the botanist said, "Did you leave your shoes behind?"

"I'm not a big fan of shoes," Fern said. "They make me feel sort of inside out and backwards."

"There's no need for shoes here – you can be as

wild as you like in my garden, Fern. My great-great grandfather built this hotel, you know. He was a rather scurrilous rogue called Solomon Silk, who, like many in his day, got his fortune by making the lives of those who worked for him an utter misery."

She gestured at the building and in a sweeping arc at the garden. "This hotel was built from the sweat and blood of everyone except him. But my grandfather was nothing like his ancestor – he was a peaceful man, a passionate gardener. Under his ownership this garden was a wild oasis in the middle of a busy city, open for anyone who wanted to take a break in their day, whether they could afford to pay for a cup of tea or not. I grew up out here in the garden or up in the glasshouse amongst the sun-loving plants, watched over by Grandpa and ignored by my parents, which suited us all perfectly."

Then Oleander's face stiffened. "If he had known what was to come, he would have lost his temper for the only time in his life." She paused, as if her thoughts pained her and then she wiped her hand across her head.

She called back into the lobby. "Ginkgo! Fetch a juice for my guest and I."

There was loud muttering in reply.

"You will have to excuse him, he is prone to strong emotions. And he's rather … protective of me." Fern had no wish to see Ginkgo's strong emotions again; her head still hurt from where he had pulled her hair so violently. The sound of a knife thwacking angrily onto a wooden board made her jump, followed by a loud whizzing noise, and then Ginkgo reappeared, carrying two glasses of grass-coloured juice that clinked with ice cubes. He handed Oleander hers and then pushed one roughly in Fern's direction.

"Apples, lemons, celery, ginger, kale, cucumber; all grown here at the hotel." Oleander said with satisfaction. "It's important to keep your chlorophyll levels up."

She drained her glass in one and licked her lips, showing teeth that looked more than a little green themselves. Fern looked at her own glass anxiously, swirling the thick juice around and around in the hope that it might go away. She wasn't particularly keen on vegetables as a rule. Then, realizing that she might be seen as rude, she took a nervous sip and was surprised to find that it was sweet, with just a tickle of spice. She sipped again, and then again.

"Now, shall we begin our tour?" Oleander stood up, stretching out the creases in the legs of her overalls.

They spent several happy hours exploring the tangled hotel garden. Oleander was always busy, prodding at new growth here, assessing shoots there, pausing now and again to trim something or take a cutting. She showed Fern how she had grafted plants together, handling them as gently as a surgeon. Fern looked at every single plant, but she saw nothing that looked anything like Special, and none of these plants, beautiful as they were, seemed to understand her.

"Now, it's time for you to see my vegetable patch – I think you might enjoy some of my edible hybrids."

She took a pair of secateurs from a leather tool belt and clipped at some stray branches. They walked through the opening she created into a small clearing. Oleander paused and looked proudly at the plants that sprouted from a collection of brightly coloured containers.

"Hybridization is the crossing of different types of plants, as you must know from identifying my prototype. Grandpa was always cross-pollinating different tomato plants, trying to create the most delicious fruits imaginable for his beloved guests. His garden provided salads and fruits and herbs for the hotel, you see, and his chefs would create the best food in London."

Oleander walked over to a large plant held up by pieces of string attached to a bamboo pole, and plucked a scarlet-and-black striped tomato from it.

"This is a direct descendent of Grandpa's invention, *Solanum Lycopersicum x Magnolia*. I have harvested seeds from them for many years to try and keep the heritage going – I think he would be pleased with the results." She cupped the tomato in her hands as if it were one of the crown jewels and handed it to Fern. "Go on, try it."

The tomato exploded its sweetness into Fern's mouth and little pips got caught up in her teeth like plankton in a whale's baleen.

"Delicious," she said, scooping them out with her tongue. Oleander smiled.

"He crossed hundreds of different varieties until he created one he was happy with. He was a perfectionist, you see, he would never give up, not until the end." She paused for a moment. "He died when I was hardly older than you." A shadow seemed to pass across her face and she moved her head gently from side to side as if trying to shake away a memory.

"Over here, let me show you some of my other creations – the cabbageberry first, I think." Crouching down, she pointed into an old oil can in which an electric red fruit lay, the size and shape of a mango. "I crossed a particularly nutritious form of cabbage with a tasty native strawberry to make cabbage that children might actually want to eat." She plucked one from the ground, then layered back a leaf and gave it to Fern. "Tell me what you think."

Fern nibbled the end of it gently and was relieved when she felt the sweet taste of strawberry on her tongue. She couldn't help taking another bite and another one, and Oleander laughed.

"You should sell these. I would buy them, every day if I could."

"My work is for my own amusement really, but I am so glad that you like them. Now, if you look at that tray of seedlings over there you will see the first stage of a trial to grow spinberries – blueberries crossed with spinach. And over there in Grandpa's old wellington boot I planted a caulipple which I am hoping will be as sweet as a cox's apple with the shape and nutrition of cauliflower. It hasn't germinated yet so I am thinking I might have made a mistake somewhere along the line." She looked disappointed.

Fern listened spellbound as Oleander described all her other clever creations, letting her sample them as they went. She felt so lucky to be with someone so clever, someone who actually seemed to have the time to be with *her*. Fern's parents had been so busy that they mostly wanted her to learn about botany from books, but out here in this wild garden she felt like she was learning through her eyes and her nose and her fingers. As they walked away from the vegetable patch, through a tunnel encased in lime-coloured willow shoots, Oleander paused, fingering a single frond that had flopped down in front of her, and looked thoughtful.

"More and more the relationship between flora and fauna – that is the plant and the animal – is skewed to suit the fauna; primarily, us humans. We give little thought to living in balance with plants, more thought to what we can get from them. Bamboo to build, rattan to weave, crops to eat, jungles to slash so that we can breed even more mammals to eat. Our greed leads us to plunder more than our share from the plant world."

Fern nodded and cleared her throat. There was something she really wanted to ask. When she got Special back, she was going to need more of the mysterious plant potion, or she was going to have to learn how to make some herself. She couldn't face Special getting ill again.

"Excuse me, please." The botanist stopped in her tracks and turned around and looked at her. "I just wondered what you feed your plants – they are so … healthy. You must be very good at feeding them the right thing."

The botanist looked pleased. "What a very good question, and I am glad that you feel you can ask me.

Don't feel shy, dear, ask whatever you want. Although that, I'm afraid, is something that will have to wait – there is something truly special that I want to show you first."

CHAPTER THIRTY-FOUR

Hidden away at the end of the garden was a small building made of the same golden stone as the hotel. Inside it smelt rich and earthy. A bucket of soil sat waiting on a wooden slab beside a stack of small pots. On the wall was a sepia photograph in a frame – a small, smiling girl sitting on top of a giant pumpkin and beside her an older man leaning on a stick, his face turned towards her proudly.

"This is where I plant my seeds," said Oleander. "Some of them I germinate over there –" she pointed to a long, low windowsill on which there were more pots; rows and rows of them with tiny shoots sticking up like green candle flames – "and some of them I germinate in a … slightly different way."

"I *love* seeds," Fern said. "I have lots and lots of them in my collection, from all over the world. Well, I did have anyway."

Oleander opened a cabinet drawer and took out a small wooden box, plucking something from inside it.

"Seeds are the most special things in the entire world – the beginning of all life. Grandpa gave me a box of them before he died, with a note telling me to remember that I could grow up to be anything I wanted. Look at this one."

She held something like a flat brown tadpole between her thumb and her finger. "So small, and yet inside this seed is a genetic map that will become an entire tree, a mighty sycamore no less! Grandpa used to call them helicopter seeds." She let the seed go and it spun to the floor, landing as gently as a butterfly.

"Seeds, like any good plan, can lie in wait for many, many years. They can bide their time until the conditions are just right." She closed the seed box and drummed her fingers on the lid as if she was thinking about something that excited her. "Now, perhaps you can help me with something. It's heavy work. Do you think you can you cope?"

Fern flexed her arms.

"I'm stronger than I look. My mum says I am small but mighty."

Oleander laughed. "I'm glad to hear it." She opened another drawer in the cabinet and took out an iron key, slotting it into a wooden door in the wall, and when it unclicked, she pulled it towards her. Fern saw that there was another door behind it, this one smooth and white, and as it slid open she was hit with an unexpected blast of cold air.

Walking towards it she felt a chill begin to wrap itself around her body. Behind the door there was a mist and as it cleared Fern saw icicles hanging from the ceiling of a long white room.

"My seed freezer," said Oleander. "Other people collect stamps or ornaments, but I collect seeds. They lie here dormant at just the right temperature."

"I didn't know you could freeze seeds!"

"Of course you can. In the wild seeds can be frozen in ice for hundreds of years and then go on to become plants. What do you think? Shall we wake them up?" Her eyes were as wide as a child about to start their favourite game.

"Yes, please!" Fern said, drawn in by Oleander's excitement. She felt her arm being grabbed and then she was pulled into the freezer and the cold quite took her breath away. Then she saw the mountain of seeds, taller than she was.

"Are these for your vegetable hybrid collection?" she said, her chilled breath curling away from her like wispy smoke.

"No, Fern, these are part of a little environmental project I am involved in." She disappeared back into the potting shed and came back with a shovel. "I need a whole wheelbarrow full – do you think you can manage?"

The wheelbarrow that Oleander produced was very deep, and Fern set to work. The seeds were all different – some flat and oblong, some as large and rounded as a walnut, others so tiny that they were just pinhead specks between the larger ones. She fell into a rhythm, but her arms began to ache long before the wheelbarrow was full and her body seemed to be sweating and freezing at the same time.

Oleander had disappeared, saying she needed to fetch petrol. Perhaps she was planning on using the lawn mower, although Fern was sure she had seen a dormouse nest peeking out from the grass, so it can't have been mown in a long time.

Finally, the wheelbarrow was full and Oleander reappeared, looking pleased with how quickly she had worked.

"Where are we taking them?"

"This way, please. Bring the shovel." Oleander pushed the barrow through an arch in a towering laburnum hedge and onto the hotel's tennis court. The net had long ago rotted away, the lines were smudged and the surface was covered by scraggy weeds, but in the middle, gleaming like a beacon, was a helicopter. It was small, almost toy-like, and painted the dark grey of a night sky with streaks of yellow down the side. Its windows were curved like insect's eyes and, under the main body, there were two fat black barrels.

"Are those … *guns*?" Fern asked, the inside of her mouth drying out.

"They are indeed," said Oleander, clicking her knuckles one at a time.

CHAPTER THIRTY-FIVE

She looked amused at the sight of Fern's face.

"Seed guns. As I fly, I shoot seeds. A one-woman pollinator. Or a human bee, perhaps."

"You plant seeds from a *helicopter*?" Fern had to say it out loud to believe it.

"Of course, and then I dose the seeds with one of my plant potions." She pointed to a metal pipe with tiny holes in it running down the main chassis. "My design was based on crop planes that work on the huge arable farms of Australia. She's loaded up with two kegs of powdered green potion in the back, so all that is left to do is to get these seeds on board." She patted the helicopter's side fondly, as if it were a pet.

Fern watched as Oleander inserted a funnel into a hidden hatch and began to pour the seeds into it. Where was she going to plant all of these seeds? The hotel had a big garden, much bigger than Fern could have imagined there to be in the middle of London, but surely it wasn't big enough to need a helicopter?

As the last of the seeds slid down the funnel Oleander leaned back on her shovel, pointing her nose to the sky where the faint outline of the moon was appearing, like the first sketch of an artist on a blank page.

"The old lady is going to be big and beautiful tonight. I follow the practice of biodynamic gardening, you see – it follows the natural rhythms of the earth and the moon. A full moon means a better gravitational pull on the plants, it gives them an extra head start. No cloud cover either, so I should have a great view across the whole city."

There was an almighty *clunk* in Fern's brain. A question danced on her lips, and although she tried not to ask it, it came out anyway, like toothpaste splurging from a tube.

"You're the Guerilla Gardener, aren't you? The one who's planting things all over the city. The one in the newspapers and the radio."

To her relief Oleander didn't look angry or surprised.

"Of *course* I am. I rather like the name that London has chosen for me, although I have always thought of myself more as a rewilder than a plant terrorist."

"But the newspapers think you're a man," Fern said.

Oleander laughed. "Why? Because the plants are so big? Or maybe because the planting has been so successful? There are many ways you can be strong, Fern, and I happen to be strong in a very important way – in here." She tapped her head. "If you germinate your brains properly the world is yours for the taking, don't forget that." It was the sort of thing her dad might have said, but somehow from this amazing woman it made Fern want to stand a little taller and prouder. She bent down into the wheelbarrow and lifted out a seed that looked like a squashed love heart with faint black squiggles running down it.

"Is this seed going to become an enormous plant?" It was hard to believe something so tiny would grow so big.

"Indeed it is. I have travelled the globe looking for the largest and fittest parent plants, to ensure that the plants I produce from them have potential for extreme growth." She licked her lips at the prospect. "Then I feed them my giant-gro plant potion and they germinate *instantly* and quickly grow to their full, tremendous potential. I make all the plant potions myself. Home-made is always best."

Her lips curled up as if she was amused by something she had said, then she climbed into the helicopter and started to check a line of switches.

Fern had a moment to gather her thoughts. Oleander was incredible and she must think that her guerilla gardening was the best thing for London. But Fern couldn't help also thinking about the people she cared about. How was Woody going to feel about *even more* plants? The wilder London got, the more he was going to feel out of control, and the more out of control he felt, the more scared he would be. Would he ever leave the house again? Uncle Ned might stop going to the libraries altogether in case of more earthquakes, and he *loved* his trips to the library.

Finally her thoughts turned to her parents. What would they have said about this? They had often talked to her about the importance of harmony, that species had to be balanced to exist and thrive. Oleander's plans didn't feel very balanced, they felt like they were all about the plants, almost as if she didn't think too much about people.

Fern's mind was made up. It felt like it was her duty to say something, and she rolled back her shoulders back to give her courage, then cleared her throat nervously.

"Don't you think that maybe … you have planted enough already? People are… People are worried about the city. Things are getting damaged. People are getting hurt. I mean… I am sure you didn't mean for that to happen, but the plants are … well, they're so big – because you are so clever of course. But because they are so big, they are causing harm."

Something told her that Oleander was a person who needed to be told how wonderful she was at every possible moment.

There was a flicker in Oleander's cheek like one of her muscles was spasming.

"People are *worried,* are they? Then their worry is pointed in the wrong direction, isn't it?"

"What do you mean?"

"There is talk of planting forests, of re-greening spaces, but that's all it is: *talk.* I decided some time ago that if you want a job done properly, you do it yourself. I am simply helping London to become a little greener again." She turned and her eyes flashed as iridescent as a beetle's back. "Can you blame me for that, Fern?" She turned to the switches again, her shoulders tensed in annoyance.

Fern thought about this. It made sense, didn't it? The world *did* need to be greener, everyone was always saying so – even the politicians were saying that now.

"Have you been up close to any of my giant creations?" Oleander voice was calmer when she turned around for the second time, and Fern shook her head.

"I've seen lots of photos in my uncle's *Grapevine.*"

"Photographs don't begin to do them justice. You should come with me. They look quite spectacular from the air."

The sun was starting to lower itself from its sky perch now and the moon was growing bolder. Was it that really that late? Fern should be heading home – Uncle Ned would have woken up and been wondering where she was. She had no idea how long it would take to get back to Dandelion Road. Perhaps she could ask Oleander if she could come again tomorrow, and then she could talk to her seriously about Special. One more night apart wouldn't matter if it meant that they could have forever together after that.

"Fly with me, Fern. I know you love plants like I do. We are so similar, you and I." For a moment she looked like the little girl who had sat happily on a pumpkin with her grandpa.

Fern had been on hundreds of planes, plenty of boats, but never in a helicopter. And to see those enormous plants up close…

"I'm with you," she said, tugging nervously on the strap of her plant-hunting bag.

"Fantastic!" Oleander threw Fern a leather hat with ear flaps. "Put this on, it gets noisy in here." She took up another hat and fitted it over her headscarf.

Fern felt a familiar surge of excitement. It wasn't climbing, but she was going up, and up was where she most liked to be.

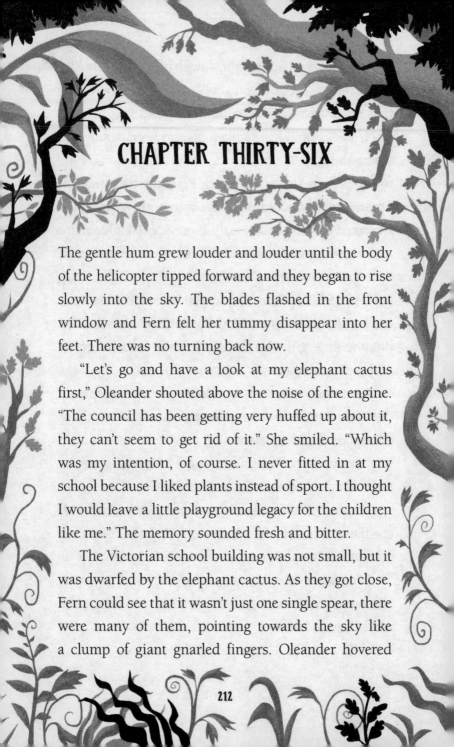

CHAPTER THIRTY-SIX

The gentle hum grew louder and louder until the body of the helicopter tipped forward and they began to rise slowly into the sky. The blades flashed in the front window and Fern felt her tummy disappear into her feet. There was no turning back now.

"Let's go and have a look at my elephant cactus first," Oleander shouted above the noise of the engine. "The council has been getting very huffed up about it, they can't seem to get rid of it." She smiled. "Which was my intention, of course. I never fitted in at my school because I liked plants instead of sport. I thought I would leave a little playground legacy for the children like me." The memory sounded fresh and bitter.

The Victorian school building was not small, but it was dwarfed by the elephant cactus. As they got close, Fern could see that it wasn't just one single spear, there were many of them, pointing towards the sky like a clump of giant gnarled fingers. Oleander hovered the helicopter next to it and they hung in the air like a bee eyeing up a flower. Fern could see clusters of spikes all over the spears, some of them as long as a car and all of them glinting fearsome and sharp in the moonlight.

"It is a magnificent example of its genus, isn't it? Even I didn't think it would grow to quite that size. Do you like it?"

Fern nodded, struck dumb by the sheer size of the cactus. Oleander's plant potion must be very powerful.

As the helicopter slipped upwards, and dusk became dark, the lights of the city turned to a carpet of glow bugs below them. They were quiet as Oleander concentrated on flying, moving the joystick gently to the left and to the right, and then the lights below them disappeared again.

"We are over Hyde Park, one of London's largest green spaces and perfect for our first dump." She began to lower the helicopter. "In nature, seeds hitchhike on other things – clothes, the fur of animals – and they often have hooks on them, to attach themselves. But we are just going to blast these babies to the ground!" She was clearly enjoying herself. "Behind you there is a red lever and when I give the word, I want you to pull on it. Pull it hard."

Fern undid her seat belt and scrabbled into the back. She found the lever and grabbed hold of it, readying herself.

"Three … two … one… Go!" shouted Oleander, slowing the helicopter right down. Fern pulled on the lever with both hands but it was stiff and refused to budge. She gave another heave, wrenching it towards her, and this time there was a noise like thousands of slingshots as the seeds were released into the gun barrels.

"Here we go!" Oleander shouted with glee, slamming the joystick so that the helicopter sprang forward, and Fern saw a stream of seeds shooting out behind them, like luminous confetti into the sky. They circled the park, criss-crossing the water, and then she slid them to a stop and spun around in a complete circle.

"Let's give them their first feed, shall we?" Oleander guided the helicopter forward again and pressed a button on the control panel. The plant potion fell like a sea mist towards the ground.

"You're a great wingman, Fern, I don't know how I ever managed without you," the botanist said, arching them round to the right. "Kensington Gardens next. Perhaps we can sow a few plants for Peter Pan to enjoy."

There was a strong smell of plant potion and petrol in the back, and as the wind picked up and the helicopter bobbed from side to side, Fern began to feel a bit sick.

"Do you know what the time is? It's just… I think I should probably be getting home."

"Has your uncle taken you to see Big Ben yet?"

"No, he is very busy," Fern said. "We're going to do the sights soon, though."

"How would anyone be too busy for a wonderful child like you? Let's go and take a look, shall we? We can find out the time then."

CHAPTER THIRTY-SEVEN

As the white clock face of Big Ben appeared out of the dark, the wind scuttled the clouds away, and the full moon emerged behind it so low and so large that it looked like the top of the clock tower was piercing it.

"Imagine what it has seen since 1859," said Oleander. "My father used to bring me here every year on my birthday. It was the only thing we ever did together. He was horologically inclined, you see; he loved to collect expensive clocks and watches."

Fern looked in wonder at the tall clock tower. She had seen it so many times in books, but never dreamed she would get this close.

"He would buy me an ice-cream from the van there and make me stand and look up at the clock. He would say, 'Kings come and go, politicians rise and fall, but Big Ben keeps on ticking.' Well, perhaps not." Oleander's upper lip curled. "Can you see my little embellishment down there? Lean a little closer."

Fern pushed her face as close as she could to the helicopter's window and saw a wiry plant had twisted up the tower and then circled itself around the great clock hands, like pretty green ribbons on a present.

"It's poison ivy, a most scurrilous plant."

"What about the bells, won't they chime any more?"

Oleander shook her head. "They have been silenced. People will be shocked tomorrow when they wake and hear no bells, but then perhaps a shock is what people need. I have made time stand still in London," she said delightedly. "Proving my father wrong. And soon, perhaps, I will make time go backwards, to when London was just water meadows."

Fern felt jolted. What did she mean? She looked at Oleander. It was only the moon that was making her face look a bit evil, that was all. The moon could do that to a face, bring shadows where there wouldn't normally be any, make it look ghostly green.

"Just over the river, you can see the London Eye, I've put a stop to that too." Fern saw the huge wheel, its capsules moving ever so slightly in the bulging wind, and her thoughts swarmed like bees. The giant plants were amazing, they were spectacular, incredible. But so was London. And like Woody and Blossom and Uncle Ned, she didn't want London to be ruined.

"Over there, look! The Tate Modern! I used

tangleweed to decorate it. You can see it rising up the central chimney – such pretty flowers. They will drop rather artistically into the Thames when the flowering season is over. Such a dramatic display seemed appropriate for an art gallery."

"How did you start your rewilding?" Fern suddenly felt a need to understand more about why Oleander was doing all of this. The botanist sighed softly, eyes looking out the front window and down at the city far below them.

"When my grandfather died, my parents inherited the Magnolia Hotel and they began to throw the most famous parties in the whole of London. Extravagant, exclusive parties that people would fly from all over the world to attend; an invitation was like being given a golden ticket. Father quickly emptied the hotel's famous wine cellar, and my mother had two dresses made for every party so that she could wear the one most suited to her mood on the day."

"Did you go to the parties too?" asked Fern. She had never been to a party, and she had always thought that they sounded like great fun.

Oleander shook her head. "I was a tremendous disappointment to my parents. They wanted an English rose for a daughter who would decorate their ballroom wearing satins and silks, greeting their party guests with polite conversation. But I was more of a thorn than a flower. I only wanted to be with my plants and learn about science. I suppose they didn't understand me and I didn't understand them."

There was a sudden *bump* on the left of the helicopter and it pitched to the side.

"It looks like the moon is bringing a storm in, the tides must be shifting the weather." Oleander looked at one of the helicopter's dials and then pressed a button.

"What about your parents? Did they come round?" said Fern. She had a picture of them in her head, delicate and dazzling like orchid plants. Oleander sighed again as if it troubled her to think about them.

"I came back from school one day to find they'd ripped out the whole garden to turn it into a dance floor so the guests wouldn't damage their shoes. They had made a bonfire and thrown all of Grandpa's plants on to it. I'll never forget the smell of smoke; the smell of the death of someone's life work." She paused, clearly in pain. "Then Grandpa's potting shed became a bar with waitresses serving gaudy cocktails. I swore that day that the moment the Magnolia Hotel became mine, I would bring Grandpa's wild back. I retreated from them, spending time in my own secret spaces where I managed to tend a few of Grandpa's plants that they had missed in their pillaging."

As the helicopter dipped, Fern's stomach did a belly flop. Oleander was lost in her thoughts and seemed not to notice that the wind was getting stronger and stronger.

"As soon as I was old enough, I went away and became a botanist, travelling the world until the hotel passed to me. Father and Mother had bankrupted themselves by then, and the hotel had fallen slowly to ruin. It took time but I brought the garden back to its wildness, and as I saw it flourish, so my ambitions grew larger. By then I had been all over the world and seen what people had done to plants, how they had abused them for their own purposes, stamped them out, paved over them – and so I knew that I wanted to bring back the wild not just to the hotel, but to the whole city."

There was a huge *bump* and Fern was thrown sideways, knocking into the chassis and jarring her knee. Sitting up, she saw that Oleander's hat had fallen from her head, taking the calico scarf with it. Fern saw the botanist's hair for the first time; it was green, the colour of wet river weed.

"I see you are admiring my hair. I think it suits me, don't you? All the chlorophyll does wonderful things for its condition."

As Fern stared at Oleander, the wind howled around

them like a collection of werewolves, and the rain beat a rhythm on the thin metal roof. As another gust hit the helicopter, it lurched out of control and began to roll, nosediving towards the river. An alarm sounded from somewhere and Oleander's hand froze in fear on the joystick. Everything seemed to slow as they spun, until time stood as still as Big Ben's clock hands.

CHAPTER THIRTY-EIGHT

The helicopter's lights were reflected back at them from the surface of the river. As Fern braced herself for the crash, she felt veins pulsing in her neck and heard a strange whooshing noise in her ears. But when the hit came, there was no splash. Instead, the lights lit up the vast green spread of a giant lily pad, and the helicopter was bouncing into the air again, tail first. It might have been fun if it hadn't been so totally terrifying.

As they fired backwards, they found themselves heading towards a plant growing out of the grey dome of St Paul's Cathedral. Fern knew this plant from Bert Beetle's book; she had read about the men who had trekked up a mountain in the Pacific and discovered it – one of the biggest carnivorous plants in the world.

"It's an Attenborough's pitcher plant!" she cried. And this was a giant version!

Oleander came out of her trance for a second. "*Nepenthes attenboroughii*. A spectacular specimen.

Thousands could get trapped inside it. At least, that is my ambition."

The helicopter ricocheted into the top of the plant and then tipped downwards and into its purple spotted pitcher. Fern saw the lid closing on them and heard a terrible, squelching *snap*. It was pitch black but the helicopter's lights illuminated a pool of dark liquid below them, filled with squirming bugs and birds that had fallen in too.

She heard a seagull, wings flapping in panic as it tried to raise itself from the liquid, its horrified call echoing back at them. The sight of it desperately fighting for its life struck terror into Fern.

They could die here. They could dissolve in the plant's guts and no one would ever know. She had to do something, and quickly.

She turned to Oleander but the botanist was rigid, her knuckles white as she clung to the dashboard. If she wasn't going to save them, Fern had to do it herself.

Elbowing her aside, she fitted her own hand on the joystick. It felt like she was touching a living thing, vibrating with life. She rammed it fowards. Up. They needed to go up. And out.

For a moment, nothing happened. Then, slowly, the helicopter's nose tilted and they began to climb.

But how was she going to get the plant to open its lid?

Aiming for the side of the pitcher, Fern let the rotary blade graze against it. The plant began to shake as if it had been tickled. She did it again, and this time the pitcher writhed around. One more time and she began to lose hope – she felt like she couldn't stay inside this horrible plant a minute longer.

Suddenly the pitcher lurched, as if the plant was sneezing. The lid opened, flooding them in moonlight. With one last shudder, the gargantuan plant shot them back into the waiting sky.

Fern whooped and steered them away quickly from the cathedral.

"Rather *dramatic*, my carnivorous collection, aren't they?"

Oleander was coming back to life.

"We could have died in there." Now that they were safe Fern's body had started to tremble all over.

"I suppose many a scientist has lost their life for the greater good of research – but I'm rather glad our names won't be added to that list. Now, give me back my joystick please."

Oleander steered them higher and higher until the buildings were small again, and then they began their descent towards the Magnolia Hotel, the wind from the helicopter's blades stirring up the weeds on the tennis court into waves.

Twisting to watch the approaching ground out of the window, Oleander skilfully guided the helicopter towards its landing. Fern looked nervously at her face, which was tinted green in a way she now knew wasn't the light. She had to get away from the botanist – whatever Oleander's talents, she was going much too far. She had to get away from this madness, before it sucked her in.

Fern had one chance, but it was a tiny one, and it was a dangerous one. Jumping forward, she swiftly rolled towards the door and grabbed the handle. Oleander startled at the movement, then her face turned angry as she realized what was happening, but with the helicopter so close to landing there was nothing she could do. The door slid open and the wind slapped Fern in the face. As the helicopter began to sway, Oleander roared with fury.

"Sit down, you will kill us both!" The ground was still a few metres away, but Fern couldn't afford to wait. She lowered her feet onto the helicopter's landing skids, feeling them thrum. Letting go of the joystick with one hand Oleander leaned as far as she could, grabbing the collar of Fern's T-shirt.

Glancing up at the moon for strength, Fern jumped, hearing a rip as the thin cotton tore. She fell awkwardly and crumpled to her knees. The landing skids were coming down on top of her now, and she flung herself out of their way, just missing being crushed. As she stood, her knees and ankles throbbed, but there was no time to see if anything was broken; if Oleander had been cross before, she was going to be raging now.

As the helicopter touched to the floor it felt like the blades were trying to pull her back into their wind tunnel, but as lightening sparked the sky, Fern ran. She ran and she didn't look back.

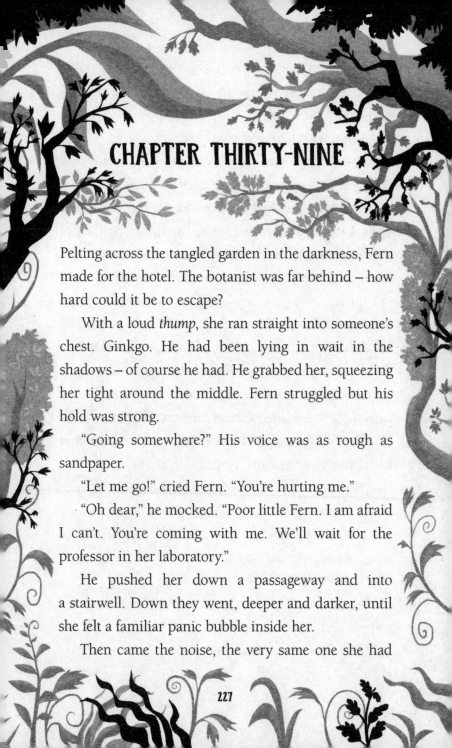

CHAPTER THIRTY-NINE

Pelting across the tangled garden in the darkness, Fern made for the hotel. The botanist was far behind – how hard could it be to escape?

With a loud *thump*, she ran straight into someone's chest. Ginkgo. He had been lying in wait in the shadows – of course he had. He grabbed her, squeezing her tight around the middle. Fern struggled but his hold was strong.

"Going somewhere?" His voice was as rough as sandpaper.

"Let me go!" cried Fern. "You're hurting me."

"Oh dear," he mocked. "Poor little Fern. I am afraid I can't. You're coming with me. We'll wait for the professor in her laboratory."

He pushed her down a passageway and into a stairwell. Down they went, deeper and darker, until she felt a familiar panic bubble inside her.

Then came the noise, the very same one she had

heard the first time Fern had come to the hotel. It rattled her bones, and the panic rose to her throat and gripped it tight.

"What was that?" she squeaked.

"You'll find out soon enough." The whites of Ginkgo's eyes were gleaming in the half-light.

When they reached the last step, he moved to slide open a metal door, shoving her through. The flick of a switch brought a row of sharply bright lights to life and metal work surfaces gleamed around a long room. Fern saw hundreds of glass jars lining the shelves on the wall like a sweet shop, but instead of sherbet lemons and jelly babies, they held plant parts suspended in clear liquid – flowers, hairy roots, thick bulbs and seed pods.

Ginkgo was shuffling a lab coat on over his tweed jacket. "Sit there," he said roughly, pointing to a stool.

"How tall are you?" He opened a cabinet door and took out a tape measure, quickly flicking it open.

"Not five feet yet," she said from the stool. "Why?"

"Interesting." He seemed to be doing sums in his head. "And how much do you weigh?" What were these strange questions all about?

"I don't know," she said. "Why?"

"Never you mind. You are about right by my estimations."

"About right for what?"

"You are going to play a very important part in the next stage of the professor's rewilding experiment," he said, moving away. "To think that someone like me could be involved in such a seismic moment in history..."

Fern felt a sense of dread. What was he talking about?

It was then that the botanist appeared – her hair whipped into a frenzy from the helicopter's winds, her eyes even wilder. Her clothes were splattered with oil and plant potion and there was a smear of mud across her face.

"I see you managed to detain her. I didn't think she would get far with you standing guard. Good work, Ginkgo." It was the first time Fern had heard her praise her assistant.

Oleander began to move round the room as if driven by a wild energy. "Do you like my laboratory? I dug out a basement here a few years ago – everyone is doing it in London, you know. *This* is the real heart of my research: a purpose-built place where I can progress with my genetic work without any prying eyes. Down here, I tweak, I tinker, I test."

"What... What are you doing here?" Fern said nervously.

"Do you know who Charles Darwin is?"

"Of course – my dad is named after him: Darwin Featherstone." Saying his name out loud in this horribly scary place made him seem nearby, and Fern felt stronger for a moment.

"Well, then, you may know his most famous words: *natura non facit saltum*. Do you know what that means?"

"Latin and I have never seen eye to eye," Fern said. But she remembered something. She'd seen those words before – on Special's plant tag. But where *was* Special? In all the excitement and horror of the last hours she had almost forgotten about it.

"*Nature makes no leap*. It was Darwin's belief that nature is never in a hurry to reinvent itself, that it is patient, that it sees the wisdom of taking its time." Oleander's eyes flashed. "But you see, Fern, I am impatient, I want to give plants the power *now* so that they can look after themselves. I want to give evolution a helping hand. For too long the earth's fauna has dominated, using the flora for their own purposes: to eat, to build, to burn. I knew that if I could create plants that could move then they would be better able to defend themselves against the growing power of humans. So I did. I think it is time you were introduced to these very special babies of mine, don't you?" Something in the pit of her stomach told Fern that she wasn't talking about the giant plants.

Oleander strode to the far end of the laboratory and pulled back a thick curtain as if she were opening the stage of a theatre. In the dark space beyond, Fern could see rows and rows of cages. And in the cages were plants. A large pipe ran down the ceiling, filled with the dark red potion.

"What are they?" Fern gulped. There had been nothing in *Bert Beetle's Botany for Beginners* to prepare her for identifying these.

"You have met my edible hybrids and my giant plants. These plants are the *next* stage of my rewilding experiment based on my work in the field of genetics. I am very pleased and proud to introduce you to my *deadly hybrids*."

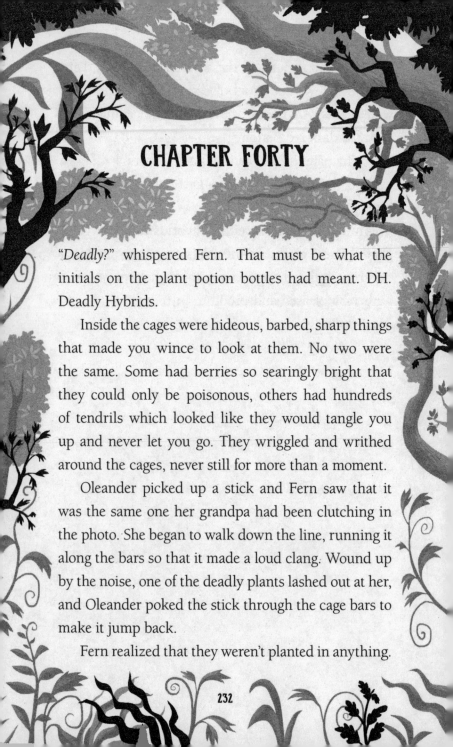

CHAPTER FORTY

"*Deadly?*" whispered Fern. That must be what the initials on the plant potion bottles had meant. DH. Deadly Hybrids.

Inside the cages were hideous, barbed, sharp things that made you wince to look at them. No two were the same. Some had berries so searingly bright that they could only be poisonous, others had hundreds of tendrils which looked like they would tangle you up and never let you go. They wriggled and writhed around the cages, never still for more than a moment.

Oleander picked up a stick and Fern saw that it was the same one her grandpa had been clutching in the photo. She began to walk down the line, running it along the bars so that it made a loud clang. Wound up by the noise, one of the deadly plants lashed out at her, and Oleander poked the stick through the cage bars to make it jump back.

Fern realized that they weren't planted in anything.

"They have no roots," she whispered, and this terrified her because she knew another plant that had no roots.

"Ten out of ten. These plants are adapted from airborne plants, so they are rootless, and also from parasitic plants like mistletoe which live off hosts such as apple trees. I always thought it strange that people like to kiss beneath a parasitic plant, but then there are many things about humankind that confuse me."

Oleander poked the stick through another one of the cage bars, and a plant lashed out at her angrily. The other plants rattled the bars in solidarity.

Fern shuddered.

"What are you going to do with them?"

"*Do* with them? They are going to swing the power back to plants, of course."

"But how?"

"Is it not clear? They have no need for soil, so they can chase people, and their parasitic genes mean they will latch onto anything nutritious they find along the way. And I rather think they might find the people of London to be very nutritious indeed."

"You mean they will…"

"Oh, yes, these plants will eat people up, Fern. They have been bred for that exact purpose. I even added a few other features I thought would be useful – a barbed prickle here, a carnivorous gene or two, anything that would help make them more deadly. Anything to help them take back London – and then, perhaps later, the world." She lifted her arms up towards the ceiling and spun in an excitable circle.

There was a pause as Fern tried to rally the thoughts that were rampaging through her head. "But you can't do this! There must be a better way for people and plants to live side by side. You can't just kill people so that plants have more space." Fern shook her fists in desperation. "I won't let you!"

"Let me? How are you planning to stop me? When I release these deadly hybrids in the city they will quickly self-pollinate and spread across London like a green virus, driving out every Londoner they meet. Then the green revolution –" the botanist's eyes glimmered – "can truly begin."

Fern looked at her in horror. Everything she'd ever believed to be great about this woman was falling away. Fern cared more about plants than most people – but this wasn't the way to save them. People had to live too.

"Now, where are my manners? Time to show you to your room at the Magnolia Hotel."

Ginkgo appeared next to Fern once more and lifted her bodily from the stool, then carried her across the laboratory into the darkest corner. He was bringing her to one of the cells – but Fern couldn't see anything in the gloomy darkness.

He shoved her inside and clanged the door shut behind her, turning the lock with a decisive *clunk*.

"You can't just lock me in here all alone!"

"Oh, but you're not alone, Fern. You have a cellmate. In fact, I believe you've met." Oleander smirked.

Fern turned around, her body trembling. Cowering at the back of the cell was a plant, clearly trying its best to stay out of the light. It looked just like Special, and yet it couldn't be, for this plant was almost as tall as Fern.

There was a thick studded collar around its middle and from this ran a chain, which was attached to the laboratory wall.

"Special? Is it you?" Fern stepped forward.

"How very foolish you were to trust me – not to see through my little scheme to make you the guinea pig for my greatest experiment yet: this prototype's first full meal."

Fern looked at Special, at her friend, who ate flies and bugs and butterflies. Surely Oleander wasn't suggesting what she seemed to be.

"No," she whispered.

"Oh, yes," Oleander said, sounding delighted. "This prototype is not just a deadly hybrid, it is a deadly *thinking* hybrid. I'm sure that you have been dying to know why."

Fern had spent so many hours wondering why Special understood her when other plants didn't. She suddenly wasn't sure she wanted to know the answer. The bedraggled scientist began to move around the laboratory again, but slower this time, almost sleepily.

"I have never been one for myths, preferring the sense of science, but during our last trip to the Amazon, Ginkgo and I visited a famous lupuna tree. The local tribes believe it contains a spirit that is the guardian of the rainforest. My curiosity was awakened and so I revisited the tree alone that night."

Fern was transfixed despite her fear. She remembered her parents telling her the myth of the lupuna tree, but she had never really believed that it could be true. It was said to contain a sacred spirit, one that protected the rainforest and punished those who were disrespectful to it. Her parents had been so careful around its beautiful, sweeping bark.

"I dug deep inside the tree and I took out a piece of its heartwood, and was amazed to find that it was glowing in my hands. I could find no scientific reasoning for this. Somehow, against my better judgement, I knew there must be something truly special about the tree."

She stopped and looked down at her hands as if the heartwood was in them, and shook her head disbelievingly.

"The next day I crumbled some of the heartwood into one of my plant potions and I chose a random hybrid from my creations to use as a control experiment. I soaked it in the potion and then I sat back and waited for it to grow. The result was beyond my wildest dreams. Right from the moment the potion touched it, it was different. The coming together of spirit and science has created the perfect intelligent killer. And now it is time to test it out."

She stopped pacing and threw back her head and laughed. Ginkgo joined in, like a horrible laughing duet.

"Special won't hurt *me*," said Fern and there was grit in her voice despite the terror in her heart. "I know it won't.

"Of course it will. Especially as you are bleeding."

Fern looked down and saw that her dungarees were ripped where she had banged her knee in the helicopter. Blood had oozed through and stained them like a blush. "They have been raised on a potion rich in blood and have a taste for killing. Best not to ask too many questions about where the blood came from, but suffice to say there are a few more Lost Pet posters in this part of the city."

Fern felt the taste of sick at the back of her mouth. Special could never get enough of the potion for its liking, so what did that mean?

"It won't eat me, it loves me." She said it even more forcefully, as much to reassure herself as to tell the professor.

"Plants are not pets, Fern. This one might understand you, but it cannot feel something as complicated as love. You can at least comfort yourself with the fact that you are helping the planet – and scientific research. I am interested to see if it strangles you or stuns you with its spike before it devours you."

Fern looked around the cage for any place where she might be able to escape, but there was none.

"They won't let you, my parents won't let you," she said, but of course nobody knew where she was. Oleander looked at her as if she was reading her like a book.

"You didn't tell anyone where you were going, did you, little Fern? How very reckless."

"Reckless." Ginkgo repeated.

"My only sadness is that I will not be here to witness my prototype at work as I have yet more planting to do from the helicopter. However, all good scientists record their findings, so I shall have to console myself with watching it back. Ginkgo! Set up the camera. I want to capture her last moments for my log."

At that moment Fern knew that Oleander was not just strange and misled; she was truly, hideously bad.

Her green eyes were radiating with the excitement of what was to come.

"You won't get away with this. Someone will stop you."

"Oh, I will, Fern, I really will. There is nobody to stop me."

She turned to her assistant. "Make sure you lock her in properly and reset the code on the door, we can't risk her raising the alarm. And set the deadly hybrids' cages to open in two hours' time. That should give me plenty of time to get back to witness their glorious first steps into the city."

Then she turned and, with green hair swishing behind her like a snake plant, she was gone.

Ginkgo's thick fingers began to spin the dial on the padlock.

"*Septum, novem, decem, sedecim*," he muttered to himself. "Oh, how clever you have become, Ginkgo, how much you have learned under her. *Septum, novem, decem, sedecim*," he said again.

There was a click as the padlock closed tight. Ginkgo looked in at her and smiled. "Scream as loud as you like, girl. I won't be able to hear you from upstairs." He turned off the light and then he was gone.

CHAPTER FORTY-ONE

Everything took on a strange shape in the semi-darkness of the laboratory – the liquid in the glass jars had a neon glow and the plants in the cages became ominous, flickering shadows. Fern shivered, suddenly cold and bone tired from all the emotion. Curling up in the corner of the cage, she clutched her knee, trying to smother the scent of blood so that the plant couldn't sense it. If she just stayed very quiet and shut her eyes, maybe nothing would happen.

Tiredness and cold fogged her brain and she couldn't tell if she was awake or asleep. The glow of the moonlit sky didn't reach the deep, dark basement, and so night could have been creeping towards day; or perhaps it had slowed itself down to witness what was going to happen to her.

But when there was a clink of metal from the back of the cage, she sat up sharply.

"Special... It's me, Fern. Are you awake?"

There was a gentle swoosh, which could have been the wing of a bat ... or a leaf moving ever so slightly.

"It's me, Fern. Your friend. Do you... Do you remember me?" She leaned a little closer to the shadow skulking at the back of the cage. "I'm the one who found you. The one who usually smells of toast." She could just make out the plant's outline and, forgetting her fear for a moment, she gasped. "I can't believe you got so big so quickly. She must have given you litres of plant potion."

A tendril, now as thick as a piece of rope, twitched ever so slightly. Fern startled. What if Oleander was right and Special *would* hurt her? With a tendril that size she wouldn't stand a chance. A truly awful thought crept into her mind. Did Special hate her now, and love the botanist instead? Is that why it wasn't responding to her?

There were things she wanted to say, things she had realized, and she was going to say them now, even if it didn't make any difference.

"Do you remember I was going to take you with me when I ran away? I've been thinking about it and, well, I don't know if I want to go any more. We've had so much fun together, haven't we? I don't think I want to leave it all behind, and I'm not sure we would have nearly as much fun on plant-hunting trips. They can be a bit hot and tiring, you see, and more than a little boring. What do you think about that, Special? Should we stay?"

The plant's tendril stayed still, though it looked as if it was shivering slightly. Special wasn't reacting to her words – and her heart felt like it was breaking. How could she make it remember her?

"I was thinking about all the silly things we have done together. Like when we played ping-pong on the kitchen table and I knocked Uncle Ned's manuscript and we had to sort all four hundred pages back in order before he woke up. It took us so long to finally track down page two-hundred-and-seventy-three underneath the fridge, do you remember?

"Then that time when Fatima Foxglove came over and her dog Fluffkins tried to wee on you and I pulled you away just in time and it went all over the floor."

As she giggled at the memory of Uncle Ned trying to use a mop for the first time, something moved in the back of the cage.One of the tendrils was coming in her direction! Every muscle in her body tightened and her nervous words carried on gushing out at top speed as it moved, ever so slowly, towards her.

"What about that time I left you for a few minutes by the spice rack and when I got back you had been investigating the turmeric and you had poured it all over yourself. We had to give you a sink-bath, do you remember? Uncle Ned could never understand why the tea towel had turned yellow. I think he blamed Garridan in the end. I wish I had told him about you, right from the start. I've been lying for so long now that I don't know how to stop. But I *am* going to stop, if I ever get out of here, that is."

Then her words ran out. The tendril had reached her toes and she drew them away sharply, moving to the far edge of the cage and pressing her back against the cold bars. Could the botanist be right? If Special was angry and hungry, then at any moment it could turn on her.

The tendril began to rise. She heard a rustling above her and saw that one of the deadly hybrids had escaped its cell and was crawling on the bars above them. Was it going to help Special to kill her?

Fern found herself starting to sing the song that her mum had taught her when she was little: a song about a coconut falling onto a beach and floating away on the sea. She could almost feel the waves lapping in her head as she sang. The tendril was brushing against her neck now and she caught its familiar smell, fresh and leafy. Then, as it started to creep down her back, she sang softly about the coconut realizing that it was a seed – a seed that could become a tree if it wanted to, just like all the other beautiful trees it had seen on its journey.

Now Special's second tendril was criss-crossing her body like it was making cat's cradle. As the coconut seed in her song broke its husk and put down roots, ready to become its own tree, Fern shut her eyes and prepared herself to feel the first fearsome crush.

But no crush came. As she finished the last lines of the song, she opened her eyes cautiously. Special's tendrils had engulfed her, but she could feel that they were hugging her as gently as if she was an egg that might crack. And it was swaying from side to side in time with her singing.

"Special! You're dancing! You do remember!"

She threw her arms around it and hugged it right back.

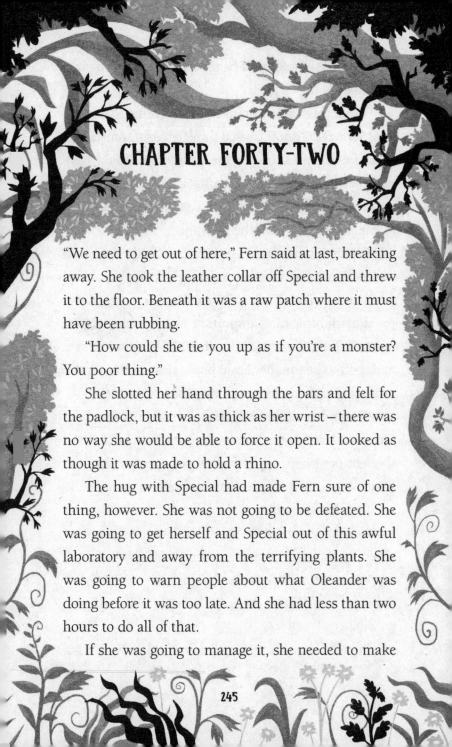

CHAPTER FORTY-TWO

"We need to get out of here," Fern said at last, breaking away. She took the leather collar off Special and threw it to the floor. Beneath it was a raw patch where it must have been rubbing.

"How could she tie you up as if you're a monster? You poor thing."

She slotted her hand through the bars and felt for the padlock, but it was as thick as her wrist – there was no way she would be able to force it open. It looked as though it was made to hold a rhino.

The hug with Special had made Fern sure of one thing, however. She was not going to be defeated. She was going to get herself and Special out of this awful laboratory and away from the terrifying plants. She was going to warn people about what Oleander was doing before it was too late. And she had less than two hours to do all of that.

If she was going to manage it, she needed to make

a plan that Woody would be proud of. But first she had to get out of this cage.

"What was it that Ginkgo was muttering to himself as he locked the door? Do you think it meant something? Maybe it was the code to the padlock. I should have been listening." She beat her fists against her forehead, and tried to cast her mind back, to imagine his horrible face as he fiddled with the padlock.

"*Septum!*" she said. "I think he said *septum*. It sounded... I just wonder... Could it be... It's sort of familiar. Is it *Latin*?" she said, aghast.

Why did this most important moment have to rest on something she found so difficult? She shut her eyes and tried to picture her Latin book, thousands of miles away (hopefully being eaten by Amazonian ants).

"A number. I think it *might* be a Latin number." She was fizzing with so much concentration that she thought her brain might pop. A picture spun into her mind of seven Roman coins and the numerals 'VII' written next to them.

"Seven!" she shouted. "It's seven. *Septum* is Latin for seven. Now, what were the other numbers? *Novem* ... *decem* ... *sedecim* ... I think *novem* is nine. And *decem* is definitely ten. *Novem, decem* ... but *sedecim* isn't eleven, so what *is* it?"

She felt a pat of encouragement on her back from

Special. She tried one more time to picture her Latin book and the Roman numerals written in it.

"Sixteen! *Sedecim* is sixteen so that is a one and a six." She spun around. "Seven, nine, ten, sixteen. I'm going to put those numbers into the padlock." She turned each one of the five dials, fingers trembling, then she tried the lock. It didn't open.

"I was wrong." She felt awful. She had been so sure that she had got it. "I should have known I would never get Latin right." She let go of the padlock.

At that moment, Special's long tendril reached over her shoulder and twiddled the lock once more. Fern looked and saw that the last dial had got caught on the seven instead of the six – and as Special pulled, the padlock slid smoothly open.

Turning around, she grinned at Special. What a shame her dad wasn't there to see how good she was at Latin when she wanted to be.

"Everyone can call me Fernus Featherstonium and feed me grapes while I lie on a bed, because from now on, I am a certified Latin ace!"

Her triumphant mood couldn't last long, though. They needed to stop the deadly hybrids breaking loose and get out of here before the professor came back.

She pushed the door of the cage open and turned to Special. "Do you think you can move again? Like you did just now, only a teeny bit further? We need to get over there, you see." She pointed at the door of the laboratory which suddenly seemed like miles away.

Special nodded enthusiastically. It made a sharp jerking movement with its stem and then toppled to the side. It banged into a workbench and sent it spinning across the room, knocking over a shelf. Jars fell, glass splintered, liquid gushed out and there were pickled plant parts strewn all over the laboratory.

"Whoops!" said Fern and helped Special upright again.

Special pointed towards the laboratory door as if telling her to go alone.

"Never, never, ever. I'm not leaving here without you. You are coming with me or I'm not going at all. We are partners. We are friends."

Special shook itself in disagreement, but Fern turned away.

"Try again, but take it slower. We've got all the time you need. Well, an hour and seventeen minutes anyway."

Putting its tendrils out on either side for balance, Special tried again – and with a movement somewhere between a shuffle and a slide, it started to make its way clumsily across the laboratory floor. Fern raised a fist in celebration, feeling like a proud parent.

But halfway across the room, Fern and Special froze. The door to the laboratory was opening – was it the other deadly hybrid come to get them? Or was Ginkgo back already?

CHAPTER FORTY-THREE

Fern couldn't believe her eyes. It was Woody.

"You found us!" She couldn't believe Woody was here. He had come to find them!

"I went to Ned's to see you and apologize. I shouldn't have blamed you about Ajee and Juniper – it wasn't your fault – I was just so worried about them. But accidents happen. Ned told me about the break-in and when I went to your room to look for you, you weren't there, and somehow I knew you would have come here, because ... well, friends sense things, I suppose." He smiled shyly. "Not that I know much about being friends."

"Neither do I," Fern said.

Woody laughed and shook his head and then reached forward to give her a hug. Special peeped out from behind Fern, and for a moment she worried it was going to be jealous, like it had with Uncle Ned, but it only patted Woody gently on the head as if to say hello. Perhaps the time in the cage had made it grow up in all sorts of ways.

"Wah!" Woody cried, flinching. Then his face softened. "Is that Special? Wowzers." He didn't run away, and his breath stayed almost calm.

"How did you know I was down *here*?"

"When I arrived, I heard voices so I followed them. I know you love the botanist, Fern, but she gives me the creeps, so I jumped out of her way as she came up the stairs. Ginkgo too. I don't like the feeling of this place." He looked around warily.

"You were right about the botanist," said Fern, shaking her head. "Oleander is her name, which I know from Bert Beetle is a poisonous plant, and I don't think anyone's ever had a more perfect name. She isn't doing good things, quite the opposite."

Fern pointed to the far end of the room where the deadly hybrids were rattling the bars hungrily as if they knew it was almost freedom time. "There are some terrible plants down here, and she's planning to release them into London in less than two hours. We need to stop her, Woody."

"But what can we do?"

"Ginkgo had a box, a black box. I think that's how he was controlling the cages."

"We need to find that box, then!" said Woody.

They began to hunt but Special had caused such a huge mess that the box was nowhere to be seen.

"What if he's taken it with him?" Fern said. "We won't be able to stop them!" Woody put his hand up to stop her talking.

"Listen. Can you hear that?" There was a *tick-tock* noise coming from somewhere.

They followed the sound to the wall. It was like a clock, or a timer – ticking down the seconds. The sound grew louder and louder, and then Woody pounced, leaning over a bin. His hand dived into it and came out triumphantly, holding a slim, smooth box. It must have fallen in when Special had tumbled over.

"Can we stop it?" Fern asked anxiously.

Woody was looking at it like he did his jigsaws, his brain clearly whizzing as he surveyed the buttons. He tapped a few, experimentally at first and then with purpose. Stubbornly it kept ticking, until with one final tap there was a whirring noise, and it went quiet.

"You're amazing!" said Fern, making him blush. "Now, let's get out of this place and find some help to stop Oleander altogether." She slipped the black box into her plant-hunting bag; there was no way she was risking Ginkgo opening the cages if he came down and found them gone.

"How, though? If we go through the hotel, Ginkgo

will find us and then we'll be back down here, locked up again. He might even feed us to those ... things." Woody let himself look at them for a second before he turned away in horror.

A sound came from behind, and Fern and Woody spun around as one.

"What was that?"

"No idea."

"Over there." Woody pointed at something moving across the laboratory floor. The escaped hybrid was back! A vine as strong and fat as a concrete pipe was slithering towards them. Was it going to attack them?

"Please don't hurt us," Fern said, but the vine slid slowly on as if it hadn't heard her, stopping just before it reached Special. To their surprise, Special bent over and patted the vine gently with a tendril.

As they watched, the vine pushed itself up from the floor and towards Special's pod, and they came together as if they were two dogs sniffing each other out, wrapping themselves around each other for a brief moment. Had Special, in this awful place, somehow made a friend?

Even if the vine couldn't understand her and Woody, could it be that plants could communicate with each other? She remembered her dad telling her that trees could communicate through their roots, warning each other about dangerous fungi, about drought, about terrible heat. Maybe there were some things that people would never know about plants, maybe they were more special than people could ever understand.

Her thoughts were interrupted as the vine slunk back to the ground again and began to wind itself away from them. Where was it going? Fern and Woody watched as it reached a pillar and began to curl itself around. Each twist took it higher, and it gathered speed as it went, until…

There was a splintering crash as it hit the ceiling with all its might. First Fern could see the building's insides, wires and mortar and dust. There was another crash, which made the whole laboratory shudder, and then she could see daylight and the parked wheels of cars.

"It's found a way outside, through the foundations! Do you think it wants us to climb up it and then escape through to the street?"

"But how are we going to carry Special if we go up there?" He looked up at the hole, mouth open.

Fern smiled at Woody.

"We don't have to. Special can move itself. What do you think? Shall we try it?" Woody shut his mouth and managed to nod, although his face didn't look excited about being so close to a plant. "Stick your feet into the gaps where the leaves meet the vine," she said. "It shouldn't be too different to climbing a tree. Just don't look down!"

Woody, who had never climbed a tree, began to pull himself up cautiously, leaning his face away from the vine. Special followed, swinging up slowly, tendril by tendril. Fern came last, and found the vine so thick that she couldn't get her hands all the way around it. The leaves were huge and it was a battle not to get engulfed by them.

"I wish I had paid more attention to how Jack climbed his beanstalk," Woody called as his feet slipped yet again and he slid down towards Special, leaves thwacking him in the face. Undeterred, he scrambled up again and passed through the ceiling.

Fern was just inching herself through the crater in the ceiling when a furious roar erupted from below. This time it *was* Ginkgo!

Glancing down nervously, she saw Ginkgo's eyes take in the bottom of the vine and then travel upwards until they rested on her feet, which were dangling through the hole.

Then they moved up again, until his eyes met her own. When she saw the anger in his, she shivered.

"*What is going on here?*" he bellowed. He was gone before she could reply, and when he reappeared there was an axe in his hands and a fearsome expression on his face.

Holding it above his head, he brought the axe down on the vine, and green flesh flew from it and splattered onto the laboratory walls.

"Faster!" Fern shouted to Special and Woody. "He's trying to stop us."

It was dark as they all squeezed through the foundations of the hotel, there was hardly any space to move, and dust was cramping her lungs – but there was daylight ahead and Fern climbed quicker than she ever had before.

Then there was a final dull *thud* from the axe and the vine slackened beneath her hands. She reached for a brick to steady herself, but it dislodged and she slipped down the vine a little. She watched in dismay as the black box tumbled back down into the bowels of the hotel. But she knew she couldn't go back. With a final pull, she forced her body out onto the pavement, and then looked back down to the laboratory.

Ginkgo held the box in his hands, leering up at her. Then he turned to face the cages.

Fern nudged Woody. Something was moving on the floor behind Ginkgo. The fallen vine that had looked so lifeless a moment ago began to wind itself around his ankles. He flinched and then tried to kick it away, but the vine wasn't giving up.

As it wrapped itself around his middle, Ginkgo's face turned blotchy. Fern watched his hand, willing for him to drop the black box.

"What will it do to him, do you think?" Woody's face was fascinated and horrified in equal measure.

"If he was as cruel to the plants as he was to me, it might be taking its revenge on him, I suppose." But Ginkgo still had the black box, and Fern gasped as she saw his finger move over the button. There was a grinding sound and then...

"The cages. They're opening, Woody."

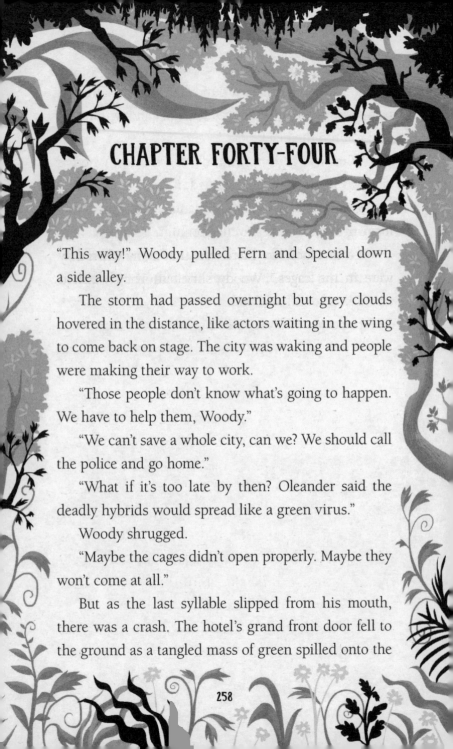

CHAPTER FORTY-FOUR

"This way!" Woody pulled Fern and Special down a side alley.

The storm had passed overnight but grey clouds hovered in the distance, like actors waiting in the wing to come back on stage. The city was waking and people were making their way to work.

"Those people don't know what's going to happen. We have to help them, Woody."

"We can't save a whole city, can we? We should call the police and go home."

"What if it's too late by then? Oleander said the deadly hybrids would spread like a green virus."

Woody shrugged.

"Maybe the cages didn't open properly. Maybe they won't come at all."

But as the last syllable slipped from his mouth, there was a crash. The hotel's grand front door fell to the ground as a tangled mass of green spilled onto the street. There was a smash as window panes broke, and more deadly hybrids pushed their way out through the splintered, rotting frames. Others appeared from gaps in the roof where tiles had long ago blown away, and one squeezed out of the chimney covered in a layer of old soot.

The deadly hybrids were free, and they were moving into the streets of London.

"It didn't look like there were that many when they were in the cages." Woody shrieked. They watched agog as one of the hybrids parted from the others and began to slink up a lamppost. It arched under its weight, smashing the glass to smithereens on the pavement below.

Fern spun around, hearing a rummaging noise coming from a metal bin behind their hiding place. A scrawny plant had climbed inside and started to sort through it, snaffling scraps of thrown-away hamburger and pizza and discarding the bits it didn't like. A walker came towards them with two dogs on leads, and as they picked up the putrid smell of the deadly hybrids they began to whine. The hybrid launched itself out of the bin at them and the dogs turned tail, pulling their owner behind them like a water skier.

"We should get out of here," said Woody as a crocodile of children walked along the pavement outside the jigsaw factory. A chunky hybrid, which had gorse flowers sticking out of its top like an old-fashioned swimming hat, ambled towards them. One of the children saw it and screamed, setting off the one behind it, until there was a line of thirty screaming children. Their panicked teacher turned to see what was going on and joined in the screaming.

Fern had seen enough.

"I'm going to do something." She began to walk out of the alley.

"What are you doing?" Woody hissed. "You'll be hurt."

"I'm not going to sit back and watch them start to hurt people. If they've been trained to chase people down, let's get them to chase *us* down. At least that way they won't chase anyone else."

"What else did Oleander say? Apart from that they would spread out and multiply."

"Do you really want to know?" Fern said, turning her face to look at him.

"Just tell me."

"She doesn't care about people, Woody, just about handing the city back to plants. The deadly hybrids can do real damage if they latch onto people, they will attach themselves to them and suck their nutrients from them. They can *kill* people, Woody."

Without waiting for his reply, Fern ran into the street and started jumping up and down, flapping her arms like a windmill. Special was right behind her, flapping its tendrils in imitation.

"Hey, you ugly lot!" she taunted. "You can't catch us. You'll never be able to move as quickly as us."

From the mess of an upturned snack van, covered in cardboard cups and coffee grounds, one of the deadly hybrids turned to look at Fern. Now that she had its attention, she started walking backwards down the street. "That's right, come and get us." She turned around and started to jog.

The lamppost climber, who appeared to be the most inquisitive of them all, and perhaps their leader, began to lumber towards them. For a moment it seemed it would be the only one to move, but then the others began to follow. There was a loud squelching sound as a plant covered in succulent leaves unstuck itself from a shop window, leaving a trail of green, slimy sap smeared across it.

Fern picked up her pace. There was a noise at her side and she startled. But when she turned to look, she saw Woody.

"Where are we going to get them to chase us to, then?'

Fern could never have imagined how happy a two-letter word like 'we' could make her feel.

"I hadn't thought about that yet."

"What did I teach you about making plans before you jump right in?"

"There wasn't any time for planning! But ... well ... what if we trap them somewhere? Somewhere they can't get out? There must be somewhere in London that is *really* strong."

"Really hard to get out of..." he repeated, and then slowed his pace just a bit so he could turn and glance at her. "Really strong," he said excitedly. "I might know the perfect place. And we're even heading in the right direction!"

"How long can we outrun them for, though?" Fern said. The hybrids were gaining on them now. "You saw how fast they came out of the hotel. What if they catch us before we get to the place that you're thinking of? If only there was some way we could move a bit quicker."

Her eyes fell on a rack full of bikes, but they were secured with chains. There were plenty of parked cars, but even if they could have broken into one, neither of them knew how to drive. Then Fern saw something else, something that might just work! Outside a takeaway shop perched a painted rickshaw – half-cycle, half-carriage, with a foldable roof like a baby's bonnet. She remembered them from countries she had visited in Asia, and they were some of the speediest things she'd ever travelled in.

"Over here!" she shouted and headed towards it, a confused Woody following after her. "You'll have to go up front, I've never ridden a bicycle before."

She jumped into the carriage, Special slid in after her, and Woody climbed onto the bicycle. As he pulled out on to the street, a row of small bells strung along the bonnet roof tinkled merrily.

"Is it working, are they still following?" Woody's legs were pumping hard but he didn't dare look back. Fern leaned out of the side and turned, then quickly faced forward again; it was like a green tidal wave behind them.

"It's working!" she shouted. She didn't tell him that it looked like the plants had already multiplied. A car pulled into the road ahead, but when the driver saw what was coming his way, he swerved, tyres screeching. As they weaved through the City, pedestrians were scattering and, as word got out, the streets emptied.

Finally, Woody slowed to a stop. He was breathing fast and his T-shirt was wet through. Special was covered in a string of pom-poms that had fallen off the rickshaw's bonnet. It looked like it was off to a party, and Fern couldn't help giggling. She looked towards Woody but his face was impassive, his gaze fixed on a bold building, enclosed by thick walls and dotted with turrets.

CHAPTER FORTY-FIVE

"Welcome to the Tower of London," said Woody, unfolding himself from the bicycle. "The most famous prison in the world. Ajee and I used to come here twice a week, I was so obsessed with it. It's held prisoners for hundreds of years and only thirty-one have ever escaped. It should be strong enough to hold the deadly hybrids too, if we can work out how to get them inside."

Caw! Caw! A big black bird landed nearby and regarded them with a sharp eye.

"The ravens!" Woody said, turning to Fern excitedly. "These are the guardians of the Tower. The legend says that there have to be six of them here all the time or else London will fall."

Fern thought that the raven looked almost as terrifying as the deadly hybrids. Woody was walking up and down, trying to squeeze out a plan.

"I once met the Ravenmaster of the Yeoman Warders and he told me the ravens are fed on blood-soaked biscuits. Maybe if we lay a trail of those biscuits the bloodthirsty hybrids might follow them, and we can lay a trap." He pointed at the solid fortress in the middle. "In there would be best; that's the White Tower."

Fern couldn't help being impressed. It seemed that history could come in very handy sometimes – as well as Latin and botany.

"I've got a map stored up here." Woody tapped his head, already running in through the front gate. "I'll try and find the Ravenmaster's stores."

Fern helped Special out of the rickshaw. The deadly hybrids were starting to arrive, and with nothing to chase they began to ransack anything they could find. They were upturning bins and chasing a terrified squirrel up a tree when Woody returned.

"No sign of him, but I found this," he said, a note of triumph in his voice. He was dragging a sack with *Corvid Food* written across it in large black letters. "You two hide and I'll start laying the trail to the White Tower. If they go for it, sneak up behind them and lock them in."

As he turned to go, Fern reached out and took him by the arm.

"Woody," she said. "You don't have to do this."

"I'm not going to let being scared define me, Fern. Not today, anyway." A dimple appeared in his left cheek, shortly followed by a matching one in his right.

"You're the bravest person I know," Fern said honestly. He batted his hand at her, but she could tell he was pleased.

Fern and Special crouched in a nook behind one of the turrets as Woody walked towards the entrance gate looking impossibly small against the centuries-old structure. He stood, feet slightly apart, on the cobbled path, then he opened the sack and took out a handful of the raven food and threw it into the air like confetti.

"Come and get it, you monsters!" he shouted, then picked up a stick and banged the metal railings.

The hybrids stopped what they were doing and turned in his direction. He began to move slowly, dropping biscuits behind him, in the direction of the White Tower. As soon as one hybrid fell upon the biscuits the others joined it, jostling each other to get to them. Fern could feel Special quaking beside her.

They waited for the last plant to pass under the ancient entrance and then she stood up. Woody's plan was working! The deadly hybrids would soon be locked away, and London would be safe.

Then she heard a ghastly noise. Twisting around she saw a deadly hybrid plant covered in raven feathers. She had a terrible suspicion that six ravens were down to five. Did that mean London was going to fall after all?

Thunder rumbled as the patiently waiting clouds began to gather themselves into action, and rain began to fall – long cold drops that lashed at her face.

She had to do something. Even one deadly hybrid on the loose was dangerous, especially if it started to multiply.

Motioning at Special to stay put, Fern ran through the cobbled tunnel beneath the entrance gate and into the green on the other side, in full view of the deadly hybrid. She began to shout and wave her hands, drawing its attention as much as she could.

In her hurry her feet muddled themselves and she fell into the wet grass, mud splattering her face. The hybrid was on her in an instant, snapping a tongue-like frond at her. She felt a clamping sensation on her foot and heard a low squelching noise as it attached itself to her.

"Get off!" she shouted. "Leave me alone." A numbing started in her toes and spread quickly up to her ankles and her legs. Then she was being dragged and bounced along the grass. She was the hybrid's prey, and it was taking her somewhere to eat her. Everything was hazy as the plant tightened its grip. She had failed. She would never see her parents again.

Somewhere in the greyness there was a familiar noise. Her foggy brain tried to place it. She felt a wind whipping at her face, the only part of her that wasn't numb, and she looked towards the noise. Something was falling from the sky towards her. She closed her eyes for a moment – and when she opened them there was a short, shrill whistle.

"Drop her!"

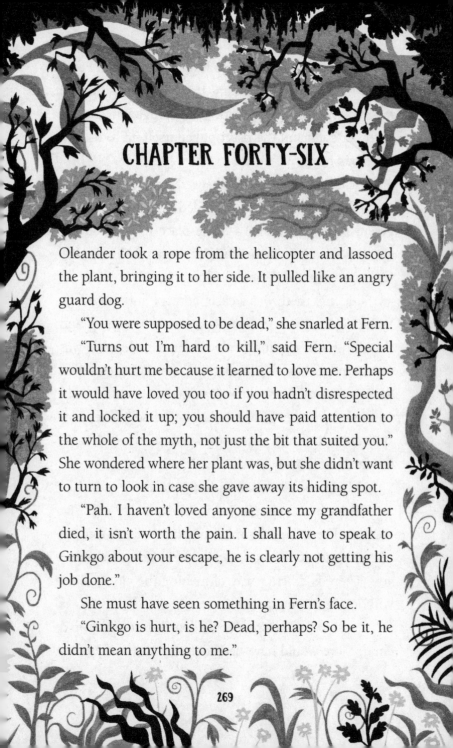

CHAPTER FORTY-SIX

Oleander took a rope from the helicopter and lassoed the plant, bringing it to her side. It pulled like an angry guard dog.

"You were supposed to be dead," she snarled at Fern.

"Turns out I'm hard to kill," said Fern. "Special wouldn't hurt me because it learned to love me. Perhaps it would have loved you too if you hadn't disrespected it and locked it up; you should have paid attention to the whole of the myth, not just the bit that suited you." She wondered where her plant was, but she didn't want to turn to look in case she gave away its hiding spot.

"Pah. I haven't loved anyone since my grandfather died, it isn't worth the pain. I shall have to speak to Ginkgo about your escape, he is clearly not getting his job done."

She must have seen something in Fern's face.

"Ginkgo is hurt, is he? Dead, perhaps? So be it, he didn't mean anything to me."

269

"You meant everything to him, though," said Fern.

"I needed a muscle man, that's all. Now, time to let this hybrid do its work." She nudged it sharply with her stick and the plant pulled itself up to its full, ferocious height.

"Please, let me go," Fern begged.

"Three queens were beheaded right here on the green. Really it's rather a noble place to go! And I'm afraid you know too much." She began to loosen the rope around the ferocious-looking plant.

Suddenly there was a cacophony of noise from the White Tower behind them – a terrible banging and thrashing and rattling of doors. Fern realized it was the sound of the deadly hybrids, finding themselves fooled. Woody must have managed to lock them in without her! She grinned despite herself. Oleander spun to look at the tower and when she turned back, her face was stormy.

"What have you done with my plants?"

"They are somewhere safe," Fern said, and she couldn't keep the triumph from her voice. "You are not going to do this to London, we're not going to let you. There is a better way of making the city greener without destroying people."

"I've told you before, people don't listen, you stupid child. More would have been done by now if they did.

You might have those specimens locked away, and you might have convinced that prototype it cannot do the job it was bred for, but it is no matter, for I have the most important component for the next generation safely in here."

Taking a small leather pouch from the pocket of her overalls she picked the leather tie open, and tipped something into her hand. Small flakes of tree heart filled it, glowing strangely luminescent against the grey of the ramparts.

"Isn't it beautiful." She tucked it back into the pouch and looked at Fern. "I am afraid you are too late. You might have captured the first generation of deadly hybrids, but the next wave will be able to think and understand. That prototype you stole serves no purpose now. If it can't kill then it is defective, an embarrassment to its kind. If I find it, I will poison it."

"Don't talk about Special like that." Fern felt a fireball of fury in the pit of her stomach. She also felt a terrible gnaw of fear; if the botanist created more plants like Special but they grew up without friendship or love – then they wouldn't end up like her friend, would they? They would be terrible, dangerous killers, much worse than the hybrids she and Woody had managed to capture.

The botanist smiled at her, triumphant in her plan.

But as the deadly hybrid spotted a raven and gave a sudden pull on the rope, Fern saw her chance. She leaped forward and pulled the pouch from Oleander's grasp – and then she ran.

There were stairs ahead, rising up to the ramparts, and she turned towards them. She was younger, faster, nimbler than Oleander; maybe she could outrun her.

At the top of the stairs, she paused – just for a second. Far below her the Thames was surging, and beyond that the Shard glinted as if it was winking encouragement at her.

"Give me back my heartwood." Oleander was close now, her face incandescent with rage.

Fern started to run again, over the uneven top of the ramparts, gaining ground. But then her heart fell. Ahead of her was a dead end. There was nowhere else to run. In an instant Oleander had caught her up.

"Ha, you didn't get far! Now give it back. It's the second time you have taken something that is mine."

Fern held the pouch high above her head, arching her back to keeping it out of Oleander's way. But as the botanist came for her, she flung the pouch and it rocketed through the sky and down towards the waiting river. As it hit the water, the pieces of heartwood flew from it and were carried away by the current, bobbing like a string of tiny fairy lights.

"No!" Oleander screamed, her body twisting in fury. She turned to Fern and, without hesitation, she released the deadly hybrid from its rope.

"Kill her," she said.

CHAPTER FORTY-SEVEN

The deadly hybrid threw itself at Fern, attaching to every bit of her body. An awful chill went straight to her bones. The haziness was coming back at the edges of her vision, but she could just make out a cloud of ravens circling above them. She strained every bit of focus she had to count them: five.

A clanking noise broke through the buzzing in her head. What was it? The raising of a gate? Were the plants breaking free? Fern saw a flash of silver behind Oleander, and it seemed to be expanding. The silver took a form and it seemed to be a person, but it didn't have a head. Was it the ghost of a guard from the White Tower come to see what was happening?

"What are you doing to my niece?" said the ghost.

"Uncle Ned!" she murmured from the grey place into which she was slipping. He wore his full suit of armour, and in his hand he carried the sword of their ancestor.

"I said, what are you doing to my niece?" His voice

sounded like it was clad in armour too. He raised the sword above his head and brought it down on the hybrid, knocking the plant to the ground. The plant was stunned for a moment before it reached for him, catching him by the ankle with a tendril and flipping him neatly onto his side with an almighty metallic clash.

But Uncle Ned was not beaten. He pulled himself up and tottered towards the hybrid.

"Nobody can overturn a Featherstone knight!" he said, raising the sword again and bringing it down to slice into the deadly hybrid.

Like a raging rhino, Oleander charged at Fern, ramming into her so that she flew through the air and landed in a breathless heap on the edge, one leg hanging off the ramparts. Lines of rage broke across the botanist's face and her eyes blazed.

"I won't let you spoil my experiment."

With the sole of her boot, she kicked Fern's other leg, and that too slipped over the edge. Her upper body followed. Gripping onto the stone, she tried to pull herself up again.

Fern looked down and then quickly back up. The ground was a long way away. She wouldn't survive if she fell.

"Please don't do this, I was only trying to do the right thing."

Oleander bent down. As her face came level with Fern's, she looked into her eyes as if she was searching for something, and Fern could smell her grassy breath. Then, reaching out one green-tipped finger, she placed it on Fern's forehead and pushed – hard.

That was all it took. Fern lost the grip of her right hand, and clung on with her left. Her weight was pulling her down. One hand couldn't hold her whole body, she knew that – not for long.

She slipped further, her body feeling impossibly heavy, just the tips of her fingers holding on.

And then there was the moment when she knew she couldn't hold on any longer. She saw Uncle Ned running towards Oleander, throwing the botanist out of the way – and as she began to fall he called her name in a terrible, sad wail.

Grey stones flashed past her, faces spiralled through her head. Her parents, Woody, Uncle Ned, Special – they spun in front of her in a kaleidoscope of colour and love. As she pointed her eyes up, not wanting to see the ground coming her way, she saw a solitary raven rising into the air; a fluffy juvenile, it must be going to take its place with the five in the sky. Six ravens. There were still six ravens. She might be done for, but London would survive.

The ground never came. She heard a swishing noise

and felt something fasten around her waist like a bull whip. She was dangling, her naked toes dancing in the space between the ground and the sky.

She looked up – and saw Special. It must have climbed the wall and attached itself to the slit of an archer's window above. It had stretched out a long, strong tendril to catch her, and it was holding her so tight her insides felt like they were rearranging themselves.

"You saved me!" she gasped with the little breath that hadn't been squeezed out of her. Then she heard another sound: the sound of the tendril that Special was holding onto the window with was stretching and beginning to rip. If Special held her weight for too long, its tendril was going to break – and they would both be done for.

"Fern!" Uncle Ned shouted. "Are you all right!" He was leaning dangerously over the parapet, swinging his sword haplessly in her direction. "I wouldn't be able to reach you even if I wasn't wearing a twenty-kilo suit of armour, I'm afraid climbing was never my bag. Will you manage?"

Fern looked up at the sheer grey wall above her and for the first time ever she wasn't sure if she could make a climb. Scaling a wall was nothing like climbing a tree. The gaps in the ancient masonry weren't big enough for a whole toe or a finger, and the gaps weren't close together either. She looked down, but that climb was even harder and longer. Then she looked at Special. Every bit of her friend was straining to keep her alive, but it couldn't hold her much longer.

"We're going up, Special," she said. "And then we are going home."

She lunged for the wall and missed, bouncing up and down like she was on the end of an elastic band. Knowing this was going to put more strain on Special's tendril, she tried again and this time managed to grab the corner of one of the stones. She swung the rest of her body after it, and as she transferred the weight to the wall, the ripping sound stopped. She paused, relieved.

Special still didn't let go. It kept its tendril around her like a climber's support rope. And as she climbed, her nose rubbing raw against the granite wall, Special followed. The rain had stopped but the stones were wet and slippery and soon every part of her body ached. Her fingertips stung like they had been whittled to just the bone. But she kept going.

Every time she stopped or couldn't find another hand hold, feeling panic flutter through her chest, she felt a nudge from below. Special was pushing her, nudging her on. Feeling its touch brought her back to her body. She could do it. She had to do it. She saw a hole to her left – it was a reach, but she could do it. She had to.

She flung her arm out and caught it, pulling herself towards Uncle Ned's face, which she could make out just above her. The visor of his helmet was up, his glasses were wonky and cracked, and he was smiling with such pride and hope that it gave her another surge of energy. A crowd had gathered, but she shut their gasps and chatter from her ears. She focused only on Special below and Uncle Ned above, and everything else she pushed from her mind. Up. She had to keep going up.

And then, finally, she had a hand in Uncle Ned's and he was pulling her over the top, and Special was coming after. They collapsed in a heap, arms and tendrils and medieval chain metal tangled together in a wonderful mess.

A troop of Tower Guards, alerted by the commotion, were standing over Oleander, their red-and-gold uniforms bright against the grey ramparts, their sharp partisan poles pointed at the botanist.

"Funny looking, isn't she?" one of them said. "Sort of green at the edges."

"You're safe!" With difficulty Uncle Ned disentangled himself and wrapped his iron arms around her, giving her a hug that took whatever wind she had left in her away. "Don't ever disappear from home again, will you, Fern? Especially to battle someone who appears to be an absolute villain of the highest order – and without even a shield in sight!"

His glasses slipped down into his visor in surprise as he saw Special lying beside them. "Goodness, isn't that the little plant you've been looking after? What? You thought I didn't know! I check on you when you are asleep every night without fail, and this little thing is always beside you. Who would have thought it could grow so big? Such a scrappy thing, it is."

The shrill wail of sirens and the flash of blue lights came now from all directions, making the ravens take to higher sky.

"Ah, good, I called the police before we left. Still, we didn't have much need for them in the end, did we?" He thumped his chest. "Good to put this to some proper use at last, it hasn't seen any action for several hundred years. What will Garridan say when I tell him? He's always saying what a wimp I am, he'll have to change his tune now! Look, can you see my trusty black steed down there?"

Fern turned her head and saw that it wasn't a horse waiting below but a black taxi with its hazard lights on. Blossom!

"How did you find me? How did you know where to look?"

"When I realized you were missing and Halo told

me that Woody had gone too, I called Blossom to take me out and search for you both. That's when she told me she had dropped you at that old jigsaw factory. After that it was only a matter of following the trail of destruction, and the rest ... well... Oh, Fern, I'm so relieved you are all right." His remarkable eyebrows danced.

As he clanked slowly to his feet. Fern turned her head towards the White Tower that had borne witness to this drama and so many before. Woody was walking away from it, a huge key in his hands and a new swagger in his step.

Then she looked over at Oleander. Her hands were being put in handcuffs behind her back, making her look strangely vulnerable, but her eyes were still raging.

"You can't hold off the plants forever," she said. "One day London *will* be wild again."

Fern looked back at Special. The plant had hardly moved, its tendrils hadn't snapped back into coils like they usually did, and its pod was hanging wearily to one side. In saving her, Special had hurt itself, and a fear struck her that the damage might be too great to survive.

"Please can we go home, Uncle Ned?" she asked and, with a great clunking sound, he nodded.

CHAPTER FORTY-EIGHT

Fern and the school shoes had temporarily parted company.

She had tried everything to make them like her. She had pounded them up and down the park, offered to deliver letters to the postbox and buy milk from the corner shop, but however far she walked in them, they felt stiff and unfriendly, squeezing her until she was all wonky and wobbly, and rubbing against her toes like sandpaper.

So, for now, she had stored them neatly in a hole in the tree trunk. Despite the fact that she now knew its name *and* its classification, it was still just her favourite tree; her thinking tree, and she had a lot of thinking to do. Its leaves were speckling orange like they had autumn pox, and through them she could see the outline of London. She loved the city even more now than she had two weeks ago. In the time since the botanist had been taken away and put into prison and the deadly hybrids had been destroyed, she and Uncle Ned had explored every last inch of it.

Fern had finally been on the London Eye (which had been cleared of monkey vine and declared safe for flight) and she had found that going upwards in an enormous wheel was almost as fun as going up powered by your own climbing feet, especially when it gave you such a good view of Buckingham Palace, which was once again flying the flag of residence now that it was safe for the Royal Family to come home. From up there she could see the Amazonian lily pads on the Thames. The mayor had decided they could stay as so many tourists were flocking to see them and using them as an extra bridge to cross the river.

The plants from the gardens and glasshouse of the Magnolia Hotel had been taken in lorries to Kew Gardens where botanists were carrying out research. Supermarkets were bidding over the rights to sell the strange hybrid fruitables Oleander had developed. Horticulturists and environmentalists and all sorts of other important '-ists' had spent hours examining the giant plants that were allowed to remain, and a company had set up tours in green, open-top buses.

And, because of the plants, the creatures had come. Birds first; plump-breasted turtle doves *turr-turr*ing from the branches of the trees, cuckoos making a racket like only grandparents could remember, and a nightingale had been heard singing in Berkley Square, which had made Uncle Ned dance around the kitchen. To the amazement of the whole city, a pair of golden eagles flew in from the glens of Scotland and built an eyrie in the towers of the Natural History Museum, fascinating the dinosaur-loving children queuing below, who went home and read all about these beautiful birds.

The river was changing too; otters were photographed playing in the Thames and cars were having to stop for toad crossings. Small acts of guerrilla gardening were popping up here and there – a wildflower garden on the side of the street, a new park made in an abandoned lot.

Sometimes Fern wondered what Oleander might think of it all from inside her prison cell. Was she happy that the people of London were encouraging their city to be a little wilder again? Or was she furious that she hadn't managed to get rid of all of the people?

Ginkgo had been found alive inside the hotel, though he hadn't gone to the police van without a fight. She wondered if they were in cells next to each other, and whether Oleander had found a way to blame Ginkgo for the failure of her plans.

The church clock across the park chimed four times, rousing Fern from her thoughts. Uncle Ned had invited their neighbours for tea and she was going to meet Woody's dad for the first time. It was time to get home. Checking her dungarees pocket to see that the *thing* was still safely inside it, she swung her legs over the branch and twisted her way downwards, stopping at the bottom to pick up her shoes and hang them round her neck by their laces. She still had four more days until school began – could she hope that they might be worn in by then?

There was a half-finished jigsaw on the step outside number sixty-seven Dandelion Road. Fern smiled. Woody had been trying to train Special to help him, but the plant kept getting overexcited and hitting the pieces all over the place. The smell of one of Halo's butter cakes baking was mushrooming out of the window and she realized lunch had been a while ago and she was hungry.

Opening the door with her key on a string, she almost tripped over a pile of papers that had blown into the hall from the kitchen like a literary torpedo. She picked them up and followed the sound of typing, passing the suit of armour which was back in its usual position, but wearing a spotty apron and with a broom resting against it.

Garridan had approached Uncle Ned with a new story idea a few days ago and he had wasted not a minute in setting it down. He was trying to retrain himself to write during the day and sleep at night and had been bashing away on the typewriter as if the story might run away from him. She put the pile of papers on the table but he didn't look up.

"Kettle's just boiled," Uncle Ned said. When she said nothing he turned to look at her.

"It came!" she said, and his face lit up to match hers. The letter had been there on the mat that morning, a colourful bird stamp gleaming out from among the bills and flyers. She had picked it up and held it close, feeling a warmth that her parents had held it in their hands not so long ago, and then put it in her dungarees pocket for safe-keeping.

"I'm almost done, just got to finish the banqueting scene," Uncle Ned said. "Garridan has rather over-indulged himself as usual and had to be taken back to his quarters in disgrace. When will he learn?" He shook his head in dismay. "Ten minutes, I promise."

Fern looked out at the tiny garden which was full of late summer colour. They had been to the garden centre by Battersea Park and filled three trolleys full of plants, and Fern had spent a day with Bert Beetle's book propped against a flowerpot, instructing her uncle on how to plant them. The cannon was still there, but it had a climber trained over it. So was the ginkgo plant, which seemed to have forgiven Fern her temper and was growing to a size that a small, not-very-hungry dinosaur might have appreciated.

She took the stairs three at a time and charged into her room.

"Special!" she called. Her plant was nowhere to be seen. Fern gripped the end of her bed in panic. What had happened? What if Ginkgo had escaped somehow and come back for it? Something featherlight touched her cheek and she looked up.

"What are you doing on the ceiling, you naughty thing!"

Special let go of the lamp shade and dropped into her arms, making her legs sag at the knees. Then she was being enveloped in a mass of tendrils and leaves and had a pod nuzzling happily into her neck, as Special moved its spike to the side so it didn't hurt her.

"Have you watered yourself today?" It shook its pod guiltily.

"Come on, then. Remember what I said."

She carried it to the bathroom and lowered it into the bath. It tugged excitedly with one of its tendrils on the pulley system that Uncle Ned had rigged up, and water gushed out of the shower head and sprinkled over it.

"That enough now, you're not an aquatic plant, you know."

Special let go of the pulley and the water stopped, and it held up its tendrils to Fern, who lifted it out and patted its leaves dry with a towel so that it didn't drip all over the floor.

She put Special down and crossed to her window where the vine from the Magnolia Hotel had twisted itself merrily around her curtain rail and hung like a green waterfall. She and Woody had managed to find it not far from the hotel, cut and torn but alive, and Blossom had bought it home for them in her taxi. It felt only right that Special had a plant friend not just a human one.

She opened the window and let in the smell of London, then let her fingers fall on the pocket of her dungarees again. She had already read the letter four times, but reading it aloud to Special would make it feel more real.

She drew it out and sat on her floor-bed, then she ran her finger under the envelope's flap, gently opening it and pulling out the thin writing paper. She held it gently in her hands if it were made of spun gold, and she began to read.

My own little Fern-bug,

I am counting down the days until I see you again. I have made a chart in the back of my logbook, and before I go to bed each night I look up at the moon and mark off a day.

We are coming to you in December, as fast as the plane will fly us. Can you imagine, a London Christmas together? An inside tree with lights instead of sleeping underneath one? Do you think Edward will cook us a turkey?

(Fern thought probably not, especially after the burned chicken incident, but she'd have to let her mum discover all about his cooking skills when she got here.)

I will go now so that we can get this taken to the town by one of our team who is leaving shortly. Your dad is agitating to take the pen from me.

Take care, my Fern-bug, not so long now.

Mummy-bug

Then, to her surprise (for he was not a letter writer), her father's stiff handwriting took over.

Dear Fern,

We have just left the rainforest and have come by boat down the Kwilu River to a city called Kikwit, where we will stay in the home of some of our colleagues. The work in the rainforest was difficult and sometimes dangerous, but the team of Congolese scientists that we have been partnered with are inspiring, and together we found some incredible new specimens. There are thousands of plants that grow only in these forests, and we have great hopes that some of the specimens will be used to help cure disease.

I know that you and I have not always seen eye to eye, particularly on the need for your application to your academic study, but your mother reminds me that I too was once a curious and mischievous young boy, although I would imagine that is as hard for you to imagine as it is for me to remember. I hope that you have managed to stay out of mischief while staying with my brother Edward. I am sure that London has very little to offer in the way of adventures, anyhow.

I must close before I run out of paper. As your mother told you, we are planning to be back with you in December, and then we will remain in London beyond that time.

You see, it appears I was rather unprepared for what it would be like without you here by our side. It seems that life is altogether gloomier without your incessant questions and playful ways. I have, it turns out, not enjoyed our work nearly so much without the constant worry that you might have broken a piece of equipment, meddled with a soil sample or engaged in communication with one of the specimens. Indeed, it appears that the only thing that has been broken in your absence is my heart, and so in a desperate attempt to mend it, I have suggested to your mother that we base ourselves in London permanently and lecture at the university about our work, with occasional forays into the wilds in the hope of finding those plants still unknown to medical science.

I hope that our new life might suit you too, Fern, for you are the specimen that matters most of all to me, and I do so want for you to flourish in the right conditions.

Work hard at your new school, Fern, and I look forward to seeing you very soon.

Your loving father,

Darwin Featherstone

Fern appeared to have developed some sort of indoor hay fever, so Special rummaged around to find her a handkerchief. She wiped her eyes dry and then tucked the letter back into her dungarees pocket where she was going to keep it close until December.

"Fern!" came a shout from downstairs. "Woody is here with his family. They appear to have brought rather a lot of cake with them."

She looked at Special and grinned. It turned out that a girl like her could be very happy in a place like this, with friends just like these.

"Race you!" she said to her plant, running for the stairs.

HOW TO MAKE
YOUR OWN SEED BOMBS

Sowing wildflowers provides vital resources to support a wide range of insects that couldn't otherwise survive in urban or built-up areas. But you don't need a helicopter to plant seed bombs! Throwing, breaking up or digging them into areas in your garden or school, or into pots or meadows, will brighten any space.

You will need:
- Meadow flower seeds or seeds collected from the garden
- Peat-free compost
- Water
- Powdered clay (found in craft shops) or clay soil
- Mixing bowl

Creating your seed bomb:

- In a large bowl, mix together one cup of seeds with five cups of compost and two to three cups of clay powder (you could use clay soil instead if you have it).
- Slowly mix in water with your hands until everything sticks together.
- Roll the mixture into firm balls.
- Leave the balls to dry in a sunny spot.
- Now for the fun bit! Plant your seed bombs by throwing them at bare parts of the garden and wait to see what pops up!

Top plants to include in your seed bombs:

Bulbous buttercup – *Ranunculus bulbosus*

Chamomile – *Chamaemelum nobile*

Common bird's-foot-trefoil – *Lotus corniculatus*

Common knapweed – *Centaurea nigra*

Common spotted-orchid – *Dactylorhiza fuchsii*

Lady's bedstraw – *Galium verum*

Red clover – *Trifolium pratense*

Wild thyme – *Thymus polytrichus*

Bert Beetle's Guide to Growing a Book

First, germinate a tiny idea.

Thank you to Clare Seymour, who loves to play with plants as much as Fern does; Kirsty Strachan, who believed in my first nervous chapters; Sophie Cheetham, who was so encouraging. Thank you also to the ladies of Learning with Nature; the wonderful Westonbirt Arboretum – those trees give off some very special vibes; and to the Royal Botanic Gardens at Kew for tending extraordinary plants that gave me so much inspiration.

Help a seedling story grow stronger.

Thank you to Imogen Cooper and the Golden Egg Academy for running a fabulous foundation course; Emma Greenwood, without whom I would never have stuck with this story; my foundie friends who became the Writing Motivation Group – meeting other people who kept notebooks to hand at all times was like an awakening. Huge shout out to Cole for Monday motivations, and to Serena, Holly, Kay, Becky, Andrew, Afroditi, Lee, Andy, Liz, Charlotte and Natalie, you talented bunch; the wonderful Write Magic community; Sarah and Dave Nelson for introducing me to the Science Park in Bristol.

Feed the story regularly.

Thank you to Lucy Hope and Clare Hawken, for lovely times at the Angel Hotel – coffee, cake, chat, repeat; my walking buddies for time spent in nature, and especially to Samantha, Tara and Ceri; Camilla Lombardi who shares my love of buying children's books.

Keep the story well-watered, especially during dry patches.

Thank you to the Manorbier Massive – David, Charlie, Huw, Ness, Maisie, Harry, Lulu, Benjy, Leo and Sebby, I love our annual pilgrimage to the Pembrokeshire sea; my American family, my inspiring sister Emily and 'WSM' Rhegan; Jamie for being a playful uncle and the most dedicated headteacher possible.

Support the story growth with a strong sturdy cane.

Thank you to Elizabeth for helping my story on its way and delicious lunches in your garden; my parents,

Roger and Jean, for houses filled with books and story tapes on car journeys; my husband Rupert, who never made me feel I should give up on writing even when I was wilting, and for cups of tea and dark chocolate; my three girls: Alice you give such insightful feedback, Izzy you wrote me encouraging messages and drew fabulous front covers, and Eliza you came up with so many thrilling plot ideas. Oh, and to Coco: you are a truly terrible terrier but having you sat at my feet is the cosiest company an author could have.

Watch in bewildered delight as it bursts into flower.

Thank you to the amazing team at Walker. Right from that first call your infectious enthusiasm made me sure I wanted to work with you. Denise Johnstone-Burt, I took off on some crazy tendril-like tangents and you gently tended me back in the right direction. You are so inspirational. Gráinne Clear, you have been so delightful to work with and your skilled grafting together of different drafts and your sprinkling of perfect words went above and beyond, I am in awe of you. Jenny Glencross, your copy-editing was the best weeding and pruning a story could have. Maia Fjord, you dreamt up a stunning cover idea, and George Ermos, you have drawn a wild delight that made me smile for three whole days when I first saw it. You are incredibly talented and I feel so blessed that Walker chose you to bring Fern and Special to life.

Disperse the seeds.

Thank you to all the teachers, parents, grandparents and carers out there who read aloud and help encourage a passion for stories in all the children out there – those who embrace reading, or those who find reading hard but love to listen. Thank you to my readers; stories and their characters will see you through life's ups and downs and open doors to so many worlds. Keep going!